The No
Wheelchair

A Novel

by
Bill Albert

MP

In memory of dear friends who taught me the joys of being a bolshy crip.

Helen Caplan

Brendan Carroll

Maureen Garnet

David Litson

Alan MacKim

Christine Mortimer

Jabuliani Ncube

Also by Bill Albert

And What About Rodríquez?

(Et Rodríquez alors?)

Desert Blues

Castle Garden

Desert Swing

Desert Requiem

Incident At Mirage Wells

Norwich 1144 A Jew's Tale

http://billalbert.me.uk

Mousehold Press

6, Constitution Opening

Norwich, NR3 4BD

www.mousehold-press.co.uk

First published by Mousehold Press in 2015

ISBN 978-1-874739-77-7

Cover by Keith Roberts and Nigel Orme

Text design by Jon Jackson

Printed by Page Bros (Norwich)

Acknowledgements

As always, my first and last loving thanks go to my wife, Gill. Without her nothing I do would be possible – literally.

Thanks also to Richard Brooks and Ajay Wagle for giving me medical advice and to Charles Davis, Rick Homberger, Mary Sykes, and Tom Shakespeare for their help, advice and encouragement.

This is a work of fiction. All names and characters are invented or used fictitiously.

Although set in a more or less real Norwich, the events and the organisations mentioned are imaginary.

Legless

The little guy in the wheelchair is stinking drunk.

"Legless," he giggles, pushing himself up to my table.

"What's that, buddy?"

Can't figure if it's the drink or the broad Norfolk accent which is giving me the most trouble.

"I'm fucking legless. Yah know, boy," he says, patting the folded ends of his empty pants legs.

"Oh sure. I gotcha."

He laughs, showing me teeth so white, so even, they must be false. English teeth for sure. His thin face is bisected by a reddened drinker's nose. It's difficult with drunks, but I figure him for mid-forties.

"Drunk, pissed, bombed, sheets in the fucking wind, or something. Right, boy?"

His wheelchair slams into the table. I reach to steady my drink.

"Yeah, OK," I say. "Take her easy there, fella."

A women comes up behind him. She is maybe half his age. Her badly-dyed black hair is lank. She wears a shapeless sweater over shapeless pants. If there has ever been a spark in her eyes, it went out some time ago.

"I'm really sorry about this. Ben's had too much…".

"Shut the fuck up, Delia, will yah. Just shut the fuck up. Christ all mighty. I gotta right, don't I? Gotta right. Sure as shit do!"

The barmaid glances over at us. Seeing that I've noticed, she turns away and lifts the glass she was drying, turning it with exaggerated care to catch the light.

"It's OK," I say to Delia. "No sweat."

"A Yank," Legless Ben crows. "A bloody Yank."

"Come on, Ben. Please? Let's not be bothering the gentleman."

"I'm not bothering nobody, am I, Yank?"

He is. In spades. I've come to the pub for a drink before going to see Dark Passage, the largely forgotten Bacall and Bogart movie and one of my dad's favorites. More than that, I've had a bad day and don't want company, especially the company of a foul-mouthed, drunken cripple, someone who's pushing three of my least favorite buttons all at the same time.

"Not really," I say, hoping I'd put enough frost on the 'really' to send the message. If not, I give him my well-practiced-tough-guy-dead-eyed stare. It usually does the business pretty good.

"See," he says, craning his head around to Delia. "I'm not bothering 'the gentleman'."

So much for the subtle inflection and the less than subtle stare. Maybe they worked at home because people had heard about my family or my rep. Here I've got neither. Here I'm just another harmless civilian.

"You know they're killing us off, don't yah, boy?" he says pointing a trembling finger at me. "One at a time. There was Janice, she was the first one. Then there was Sarah, then there was Barry. Poor bloody Barry. All fucking dead, dead as fucking parrots."

He makes a gun with his fingers and shoots me.

"Bang, bang, bang."

"Sure thing, buddy."

" 'Sure thing, buddy', sure thing my bleeding arse," he says pushing his wheelchair up closer.

"Listen, pal…".

"No, you listen, 'pal'."

"Ben, please."

He ignores her.

"Think I'm just another bloody drunk crip, don't yah, boy? Full of beer, chip on the shoulder. Sure, a crip with a chip. Ha! Maybe a bit touched in the head to boot? That what you thinking, Yank?"

"You're dead right about that, pal."

He laughs, reaches over and pats my arm. I feel the bony hardness of his hand through my jacket.

"Good. I like that. Honest that is. You know what most of them says? 'Course not', they says. 'Course not.' Then they runs away quick as they can. Not that you're about to do that on me, are you, Yank?"

"No, I guess not."

"You been in that long?" he asks, pointing at my wheelchair.

"A few months or so. Temporary kinda thing, you know."

"New boy. I figured yah straight off for a new boy."

"How's that?"

"Yah spend as long as I have using a chair, yah just know is all."

He takes a long pull at his drink.

"Sitting all kinda wrong, got new gloves there and the chair's too shiny fucking clean is what it is."

That's a problem this poor schmuck doesn't have. His chair's frame is dented, chipped and covered in stickers – "Piss on Pity", "Make my Day", "Norwich City FC". A small, scuffed yellow and green plastic sports bag dangles off the back.

"Is that it?" I ask.

"Be enough for starters, don't yah reckon?"

Why do handicapped people think they own other handicapped people? I haven't been here long enough to work it out. I'm not planning to have the time to work it out.

"Listen, buddy, I'd love to sit here and talk, but my movie is about…".

Delia grabs the back of his chair and begins to pull him away.

"What the fuck do yah think you're after doing, woman?" he shouts.

"Gentleman's gotta go, Ben. He just said."

He clamps his hands on the wheel rims. The chair stops dead.

"Figure yah know what it's all about, don't yah, Yank? All bloody Yanks think yah know everything. Know every bloody thing. Don't yah?"

I sigh. Drunks. Wheelchairs or not, they're all the same.

He leans closer and lowers his voice. His breath is sour with beer.

"Like I says, one at a time. That's right. One at a fucking time. And yah know who's next on the list?" He stabs a dirty thumb hard into his chest. "That's right, mate. Sure I am. Stands to reason that do an all."

"Don't pay him any mind, mister," Delia says. "He's upset is what it is. Some of his friends...".

"Will yah fuck off out of it, woman. I'm talking here. Yeah? Fuck it!"

The pub fills up with the silence of people not paying attention. A thin man with tired eyes comes wearily from behind the bar. He leans over the back of Ben's chair.

"You all right there, Ben?"

"Yeah, Nick. I'm good. You?"

"Just fine. I don't have to say anything now, do I, mate?"

Ben twists around.

"No," he laughs. "Less yah want to be telling her to leave me be."

"Right," the woman says, her dark eyes flaring into life. "You're so bloody independent, Benjamin Castle, push yourself home. And good bloody luck too."

She goes quickly up the three stairs which lead from the pub to the movie theatre and is gone.

He watches her go, shaking his head.

"Bloody woman. What yah gonna do, huh? Can I get

us in another round?"

"No thanks, pal."

"Speak out, they be after putting you on that list. Maybe the bastards will put you on the list too, mate. Then you'll know what I'm fucking talking about here. Wadda yah think?"

"I think I'm out of here, my friend. I gotta movie to see in a couple of minutes."

I turn my chair around and start for the side door.

"Well," he calls after me. "I'm here to tell yah, yah don't know shit, Yank. Yah don't know what it's about, any of it."

He's probably dead right about that.

Sorry

I've always disliked handicapped people. Not personally, you understand, but as a group. And it's not really dislike I feel, it's more distaste. They are just too damn close a reminder of vulnerability, decay and death. They're big time losers. Disgusting. Unpredictable. Embarrassing. Helpless. I only need to see a blind face sniffing the air, white stick tapping or stumblesurfing behind a seeing-eye dog and I'm gone. Wheelchairs? I cross the road quick as I can, quicker when the person stuck in the chair twists and squirms, trying to talk but instead can only manage dribbles and grunts. Then there's all those crazy-eyed old guys who left bits of themselves over in Vietnam and the younger ones with broken bodies and messed-up minds from the show in Iraq or the one in Afghanistan. Arms, legs, faces, minds, all gone. Terrifying, right? I figure who needs it? Not them. Not me. No, sir, for damn sure not me.

OK, you're thinking maybe I should feel sorry for them. Sure thing. I can do that. Easy. Sorry as hell. But you see 'sorry' and disgust work together pretty damn good. In fact, if you didn't feel a certain amount of disgust, quite a gigantic load of disgust, why would you feel sorry? So I guess if you cut it right down and right close, I do feel sorry for the poor bastards. It's just that I don't see why I need to feel sorry for them so damn close up and so damn personal.

All of which brings me to 'sorry'.

"I'm afraid we can't tell you, Mr. Green. The condition

is so variable and so unpredictable. I'm terribly sorry."

"That's it, you're sorry?"

The doctor took off his glasses and pinched the bridge of his nose with thumb and forefinger. He looked tired. Giving out bad news all day is a real tough business. Poor guy.

"Yours is a most unusual case, Mr. Green. Most unusual. Apart from fatigue, it appears that it's mainly the muscles in your legs that remain affected. Sudden onset ruled out such things as any of the muscle wasting diseases. The way the condition presents, as well as the tests we've carried out, strongly indicate a rather rare type of what's known as Guillain-Barré Syndrome. We were extremely fortunate that we had Dr. Ho, a visitor from Beijing, with us. Do you remember seeing him when you were on the ward? Yes? Well, he is of the opinion, and I am in agreement, that we are looking at a case of acute motor axonal neuropathy, something which is very rare in Europe, but far more common in China. The difficulty we have is that with any type of Guillain-Barré it is virtually impossible to determine when or even if you will recover completely."

My first thought was, typical socialized medicine. If I was back in the good old U S of A, Dr. Steve, our family doctor, would know who to send me to, and they'd have the answer, and quickly. If I had enough money to go to a private quack, I'm sure they'd have an answer here as well.

'Better than nothing. Better than nothing.' I repeat to myself to keep my head straight. If I was broke in LA, I'd probably still be waiting to see a doctor. Might even be dead meat by now, although sometimes I feel that's what I am. Dead meat rolling.

"So, you're telling me I have to wait and see? That's it?"

"How long has it been now?" he asked, searching the green folder of notes on his desk. "Remind me."

Just another number, like the defeated people slumped on plastic chairs or stuck in wheelchairs in the corridor outside his office.

I'd been feeling sick for a couple of weeks, lightheaded, tired, weak, with numb hands and feet. Figured it for a bad chill or a really bad cold. Then one afternoon as I was leaving the house I passed out. I woke up in the emergency room at the hospital. They rushed me to a ward, where I was hooked up to a lot of machines, examined by one head-shaking doctor after another, as one bit of me after another closed down - arms, legs, breathing. After a couple of weeks almost everything came back but my legs. I still had some feeling, but couldn't stand up, the muscles had apparently lost interest. Then there was the other problem.

"It's not at all difficult, my dear," the continence nurse had assured me. "Once you get over the psychological barrier. Of course, some men feel a little pain at first, as well as a little discomfort. But with practice, that will pass. The important thing is to relax. Think of it as a kind of sword swallowing. If you keep it straight and relax, the sword goes down without cutting your windpipe."

That didn't help at all.

"First you clean it with an antibacterial wipe. Good. Then you clean your hands. That's fine. Aren't we doing well?"

"It's not showing much interest is it?" she observed, looking down at my very clean, but shriveling-in-terror schlong. "Here, if you don't mind, let me give you a hand."

As if she was dealing with a random bit of hose, she took me in her gloved hand and shoved my flaccid cock flat against my stomach.

"I'm afraid that closing your eyes defeats the purpose, my dear. Come on now, be brave. Here take this. No? OK, not to worry. Just hold your penis for me. There. That's fine. Now I want you to relax. Can you do that for me?"

As she took a long, narrow plastic tube that she'd removed from it's plastic wrapper and held it poised above my penis, relax was a big ask. As I watched, hoping that it was happening to someone else, she inserted one end and slid it down slowly until the only thing that remained visible was a small, white, megaphone-shaped plastic nozzle. I waited for a public announcement. Instead, I felt only discomfort, but more, immense relief as a stream of urine appeared and the pressure on my bladder eased. Magic.

Although I didn't like it, I quickly got used to catheterizing three or four times a day. What else to do? No choice.

"Much better than an indwelling one, my dear.

Because you still have feeling there, it will be much more comfortable. Less chance of infection as well. And think how very lucky you are that you can still open your bowels."

Oh boy, oh boy. Lucky me.

"About two weeks, doctor, since I left the hospital that is. Something like that anyway."

"Well, that's not very long, is it? Let's say we keep on with physiotherapy and see what happens while we explore other possible solutions. How does that sound?"

"Not real encouraging."

He looked at his watch.

"I'm afraid it's the best we can do at the moment, Mr. Green. I know it's not easy, but let's look on the bright side."

"The bright side? The god-damned bright side! Give me a break here, Doc. What particular kinda bright side would that be?"

Behind me his nurse coughed.

"Well, the bright side is that you don't seem to be in much pain, and unlike almost everyone who is left unable to walk because of a spinal injury, you don't have to go for a long and demanding rehab at Addenbrookes. Furthermore, your bowels seem fine and your waterworks, well we're having a bit of a problem in that department, but…".

"Water works?" I interrupted. "That some kind of joke?"

"Not in the least, Mr. Green. Your personal plumbing? Is that better? Would you care for something more medically precise?"

I didn't reply.

"As I was going to say, everything else seems to be just fine, of course, besides passing water and your legs."

"Besides my god-damned legs? Besides having to piss through a straw? Jesus H. Christ, man! I can't piss! God damn it. I can't walk! What the hell kinda life is that?"

"Please, Mr. Green, there's no need to raise your voice or to use such language. I understand that you're feeling angry and frustrated. That's natural. Of course it is. I assure you we will do everything we can to help, but you must be patient."

My father told me that unless you can muscle them or buy them, never piss off anyone you have to depend on for something really important, especially if you don't have the expertise or can't see what they're doing. Car mechanics, waiters, roofers, insurance adjusters, and, of course, doctors.

"They've got you by the cojones, Bobby. So, no matter how mad you get, you bite it back and smile as if there's no tomorrow. If you don't, if you yell at them, they'll just go behind the door and spit in your soup."

For sure I didn't feature this guy spitting in my soup.

"Sorry," I said.

Not Swimming

"Robert Green?"

"Yeah, that's right."

He pushes a photo ID card at me. There are two of them. Cheap suits, thin ties and over-polished, heavy, black shoes.

"I'm Detective Sergeant Richards and this is DC Cornish. Need to have a brief word, Mr. Green. Mind if we come in?"

And if I do? The same all over the world, cops asking questions for which they expect only one answer. I've grown up on a steady diet of those questions. I motion them inside.

Richards, overweight and comb-over balding, looks to be in his early forties and permanently out of breath. His partner is a mousy guy. Mid twenties. More store clerk than detective.

"Not much furniture, Mr. Green," Richards observes. "Just moved in, have you?"

The door opens directly into the small front room of my council house. Besides our rolled-up futon mattresses parked against one wall - my daughter Anna and I both sleep here because I can't make the stairs and I want her as close as possible - there's a metal standing lamp, an old portable TV, a leatherette easy chair I picked up at a sort of Goodwill place on Magdalen Street, some of Anna's drawings scotch-taped to the wall and a scattering of her toys. Soon after I was taken to the hospital, my wife left, taking everything, right down to the light bulbs and the toilet paper. She'd also made off with my iPhone and all my painstakingly collected Delta and Chicago blues, the music that connected me with the heart of my former self. Worse than all that, my entire stash, more than $17,000 had vanished. Granted, it hadn't been a long or a happy marriage. I can't complain about the short or the unhappy, as she was our bought-and-paid-for ticket to dance around the British immigration laws, although there was more dancing to do before all the paperwork is nailed down tight. With Tina in the wind, that is going to be a problem. For the moment, however, I've got more urgent things on my plate – no money, no working legs and, now, a couple of nosy cops.

It's been a long and sudden drop for me, Bobby Fishbaum, the sharp dresser with a new metallic yellow 911 GT Porsche, the guy with a 60-inch flatscreen, a penthouse apartment in Santa Monica overlooking the ocean, the guy who could take care of himself and take care of business, to this - dead broke, chained to a wheelchair, having to crick my neck to talk to anyone except little kids and living in the English version of the Projects. Can't even say, "Still, I've got my health."

"I like the simple life," I say to the cops. "Besides, gives me more space to move around."

My visitors exchange detective looks.

Being a smartass is not my best move, but I can't help myself.

"An American", declares Cornish, looking pleased with his detective skills

"That's right."

"What part you from?" Richards asks as he walks to the far door and glances into the kitchen at the back.

"California."

"Big place California," he says.

This character is real sharp.

"Sure is."

But me, I am a regular razor. No one cuts it better than Bobby Fishbaum.

"How'd an American come to wind up on a council estate in Norwich?"

"My wife, she's a local girl."

"In the forces, were you?" Cornish asks. "Over to Mildenhall?"

"Your wife, the local girl, she like the simple life too?" Richards says, spreading his arms to take in the room.

Sure as hell they've rumbled our immigration scam. Tina has tipped them off. If I could buy her, she'd not be slow to sell me on. It makes perfect, cold-logic sense.

"Listen, fellas, I'm sure you have more interesting things to do than hear about my little domestic problems. Really a dull, dull story."

"Yeah," says Richards with a sigh. "I know, marriage can be a real bitch sometimes."

He pats me on the shoulder.

"Can I help you guys with something?"

Cornish walks over.

"You know this man?" he says, handing me a small photobooth photo.

The face is familiar but I can't place it.

"Can't say that I do."

"That's funny," Cornish remarks, "His wife said he spoke to you just the other night over to Cinema City."

I look at the photo again.

"OK. Yeah, right. It's him, Legless Ben. I can see it now. Not a very good likeness. Hard to recognize him without the wheelchair. Listen, I don't know the guy at all. Only ran into him for a few minutes the other night. What's he done?"

"Done? Nothing," says Richards. "Nothing we know about that is. His body was fished out of the river up near Pulls Ferry yesterday morning."

I wonder whether he was still in his wheelchair. I don't ask.

No Way to Run

Cops. I know from cops. As early as I can remember they were virtually part of the family. Coming to call at all hours. Sitting around the kitchen table drinking coffee with my father and my uncle. Sometimes they took them off for less friendly chats down at the station. When I was a kid, cops even sent me birthday cards.

"They're just like us," my father explained. "You know, regular kind of family guys. They like baseball, they like gin rummy, some even like pinochle, they got kids. It's only that they're on the other side so to speak."

The thing they were on the other side of was the law. Our family business was just the other side of almost legitimate. Like lots of Jews, my father and my uncle were in the rag trade. They didn't make clothes, they imported them, which would have been kosher if it wasn't for the designer labels which weren't kosher. From time to time they sold the genuine stuff, but that came from unofficial sources, meaning hijacked trucks or containers or warehouses where someone forgot to lock the doors, and that often meant a kitchen-table visit. It was part of the way things were.

But these cops I don't need nosing around asking questions. Our new identity is pretty damn tight, but if you start picking there is always a chance of finding a loose thread. For the people trying to find me and Anna a loose thread would be more than enough.

My mistake was to let the cops in LA talk me into

testifying against the Russian Jews who were muscling in on our business. It was strange because the new crowd was from Odessa, just like my great-grandfather, Abraham "Gefilte" Fishbaum. He'd arrived in America in the 1890s, and with the Odessa connections he soon found his vocation working a horse poisoning racket on the Lower East Side. With his son it had been Prohibition. No machine-guns and crates of whisky for Isaac "The Rabbi" Fishbaum. For him it was a sacramental wine scam with crooked rabbis and non-existent Jewish congregations. After Repeal, gambling supported the Fishbaum clan, first in New York, then Las Vegas in '49 with Bugsy Siegel and finally in LA. The designer-label business came along later on.

Although the new racket was a step up from bookmaking and a world away from horse poisoning, my father wanted something better for me. I was to be the first totally legit Fishbaum, a Fishbaum without an underworld moniker. The plan was college, maybe accounting or business administration. It never happened. Uncle Sol retired to Atlantic City and then during my first year at UCLA dad had a stroke which left him semi-comatose in a convalescent home in the Valley, where he died not long after. I, Bobby "The Fixer" Fishbaum, was the only one left to run the family business.

The Feds wanted to put me into witness protection, but I knew no program was built that could protect me or my daughter from people who made Mickey Cohen and Bugsy Siegel look like yeshiva bochurs. The Russians don't just bump off wiseguys like the old time Jewish or Italian mobs, they do whole families and they do them messy - loud and clear 'don't-mess-with-us' announcements. So I picked up Anna from my ex, telling her we'd be back on Sunday. Instead we headed to Mexico, where the family had connections who set us up with new passports. I sent Anna's mother a postcard, although addressed to one of her friends, explaining what was going down. I was sure she was going to be pissed off, but figured better that than the other. I'd been keeping her posted in a roundabout way through her friend and the Mexican contacts. Not great for her, but the best I can do right now.

From Mexico we flew to Panama. Another passport change and then on to Lima. That's where I found Tina, down to her last few bucks and desperate to get home. I got us fixed up with new passports, we got married, got visas from the embassy and then flew to England where I planned for us to fade quietly into a provincial backwater. Being linked by the cops to a dead person was not in the plan. Neither was getting stuck in this damn wheelchair and losing all my bread and the last shred of juice I had been clinging onto.

Richards takes a notepad out of the side pocket of his jacket.

"Would you be prepared to make a statement, Mr. Green?" he asks.

"How'd you guys find me?"

"That's what detectives do," laughs Richards.

"Besides," Cornish chimes in, "Norwich ain't a big place, is it? Not many wheelchair-bound Americans about neither."

I am feeling more naked by the minute.

"A statement?" Richards repeats.

"A statement about what?"

"What you talked about with Mr. Castle."

"Do you know what happened to him?" I ask.

"That's part of the ongoing investigation, although from what we understand he had had quite a lot to drink."

"You mean you think he fell in?"

"Most likely."

"Then what is the point of knowing what we talked about?"

"Police procedure, Mr. Green. That's all."

I know better, but not wanting to get them too interested in me I recount Legless Ben's story.

They both smile indulgently.

"Same old yarn that is" Cornish says when I've finished. "He come into Bethel Street after one of his mates died, going on and on about lists and that. I reckon the boy was paranoid is what it was. I mean, who in their right mind wants to be killing cripples?"

"Disabled people," Richards corrects.

Cornish shakes his head, resigned.

"Sure," I say, not in the least bit resigned. "Who the hell wants to kill cripples?"

Child's Play

I can hear the children pounding up the path. The door swings open, banging against the wall.

"Daddy! Daddy!"

Anna stops short when she sees the two cops. Her friend Harley bumps into her. Two five-year olds, big-eyed and breathless.

"Daddy?"

"It's OK, Pumpkin, these gentlemen were just about to leave."

A few seconds later Harley's mother, Molly, comes in. She looks a question at me. I shrug.

I can see the two cops trying to weigh things up. It takes some weighing. Molly is almost six feet tall and built like a linebacker. She has flame red hair in long dreadlocks, five or six earrings in each ear and tattoos on her arms. The tattoos advertise how she makes a living. Right now they are covered up by a studded, leather motorcycle jacket.

"You are?" asks Richards.

"Bloody shagged out I am," replies Molly, giving him a defiant stare.

"She's my next-door neighbor," I say, trying to fend off an incident. "Molly helps me out by taking Anna to and from school. Couple of pretty steep hills between here and there."

"Sure," he says, wisely not taking his eyes off Molly.

Anna comes over and clambers up into my lap. She puts her arms around me, at least as far around as they can reach, and holds on tight, burying her head in my chest. Being on the run has not been easy for her.

"Daddy?" she says again, her voice muffled by my sweater.

I pat her head.

"Still," Richards continues. "Gotta be tough looking after a kid with…". He gestures at me. "Well, you know what I mean."

I know what he means.

"Right," Cornish says, "We'll leave you be then, Mr. Green."

"We know where you are if we need to talk again," adds Richards.

"Mind how you go," says Cornish.

They go out through the open door, not closing it behind them. The four of us watch them walk down the path and out onto the sidewalk.

"So, what's the filth after, Greenie? You been a naughty boy, have you?"

"How'd you know they were cops?"

"Bears and woods, mate. Bears and woods."

"Teddy bears!" shouts Anna, jumping to the floor, the tension broken.

"Picnic!" finishes Harley.

Singing and laughing they run through the kitchen and into the back yard.

Anna is her mother, dark and intense. Before all this, I was a weekend dad, sometimes an every-other-weekend dad. Now, the protective intimacy, the closeness, the daily discoveries we make about each other, fill me up with a love so unimagined and so intense that it almost breaks my heart, both for the time I've lost and the pain her mother must be feeling. I'm sure Rebecca is hurting real bad, but at least she understands how this has to work. Anna? Well, of course, she doesn't.

Every night she asks me about her mom and when we're going home. To take her away from those worries and to get her to sleep, I tell her stories. Some of them are fairy stories, others are untrue.

Our story is that we needed a new last name because we are on an extra special mission for the President of the United States. As long as no one knows our real names we will be safe and so will the President. The story grows each bedtime. Luckily Anna is good with make believe and at keeping secrets.

"She OK at school today, Molly?"

"I guess. The teacher didn't say anything when she came out with them."

It is hard to believe when looking at Molly in all her tribal splendor that she studied literature at the local university. You can hear it when she speaks, but she never talks about that other country.

Her boyfriend is as startling as Molly. Centre of the line material. Six two or three, 280 and a living mural. It had been surreal seeing them with Harley at the Cathedral's Nativity Service. Even stranger than the hulking Hell's

Angel family in the middle of that so-polite English scene, had been the fact that no one else seemed perturbed. At least if they were, they didn't show it.

From Hell or wherever, these two really are my angels. When I was in the hospital they took care of Anna and since we arrived they have treated us as if we were part of their family. Who could ask anything more from angels?

"Thanks for everything, Molly. I couldn't make it without you and Paddy."

"Yeah, yeah, yeah," she replies. "You fancy a cuppa?"

"Long as it's not tea."

"Bloody Yank."

What Life?

"**Y**ou are very fortunate, my love. Very. Tell me, did you go to the gym before your illness?"

"Back home, yeah, every other day, work permitting. Makes me fortunate, does it?"

As the doctor ordered, a few weeks after I saw him I went to rehab physiotherapy. It was in a very large room filled with padded tables screened off by curtains and lots of peculiar-looking machines. Hanging on the walls were leather straps, plastic shapes, webbing, wooden rods, rubber pads, and metal objects of all shapes and sizes. If I didn't know it was a place that was supposed to make you better, I'd have guessed it was a place to make you confess your sins, spill your guts and beg for mercy.

Lucky for me, the therapist was not a sweaty, hooded guy in black leather, but a jolly middle-aged woman who carried nothing more threatening than a clipboard and a smile.

"Oh, yes, my love, very fortunate. You're going to need that strong back and those muscled arms more now. To the inexperienced eye it may seem easy to propel yourself in a wheelchair, but now you have been doing it for a few weeks, I'm sure that you can see it demands strength and endurance."

"And balance," I added.

"Oh yes, love, and balance too, lots of balance."

"I appreciate your help, Miss Younger, but how about more work on the legs? That's what I really need

31

if I want to get myself out of this damn contraption and back on my own two feet. That's what I want, more than anything."

"Of course you do. Everyone does, especially at first."

"At first?"

"I mean when they first have to use a wheelchair. It's natural, of course, but one thing at a time, love. I know it is difficult, especially with all the negative ideas you have about wheelchairs, but my advice to you is that life will be easier if you learn to treat your 'damn contraption' not as an enemy but as a friend, right now as maybe your very best friend. Think you can do that?"

Damned if I could! I wanted to explain, but figured she wouldn't understand. Back home I had earned a certain respect, essential for what I did and how I survived in my world, by being thought of as a real stand-up guy. So how does that work if you can't even stand up?

"Come on, Miss Younger, please. How can I treat this thing as a friend? I'm trapped, stuck, confined in it all day long and only escape when I go to bed. Being wheelchair bound is not how I see my life, any life really."

"What a moaning minnie!" a voice called from the other side of a blue plastic curtain. "Stop your bleating, mate. Get some backbone and just get on with it."

"Ronald, please! You know better than that."

"Of course I do, Gladys. But what that bloke needs is a stiff injection of reality and discipline, not your 'it will be alright, dear' bollocks."

"You tell 'em, Ronny," an old woman's voice cackled

out from behind another curtain.

"Off again, he is," a man joined the growing chorus. "Bleeding cheek, you've got Ronny. Bleeding cheek is what I calls it."

I expected the jovial Gladys Younger to lose the jovial and blow a gasket. Instead, and against her best efforts to stifle it, she began to laugh.

"You must forgive, Ronald, Mr. Green, and the others. I'm afraid he just can't help himself. Sets 'em all off."

I never have been, and was not then, up for forgiving a loudmouthed buttinsky. I reached over and yanked the curtain aside. Oh, holy steaming kreplach! Bad move. Glaring back at me was a dramatically emaciated guy with fiery eyes. It looked as if he was hanging from the wall. That was because of being strapped into one of the more serious pieces of machinery, which had fixed him into a standing position. Judging by the belts across his forehead, chest, waist and legs, that's the only way he had of being a stand-up guy.

"You wanna take a snap?" he asked, softly. "It'll last longer."

"Boys, no call for all this."

"Sorry, man," I said "I didn't know."

"Didn't know what, Green? What 'bound' means? That," by moving his eyes he indicated his electric wheelchair, "that there damned contraption, that is freedom. Big letters F-R-E-E-D-O-M. What you've got your disabled arse on - that's freedom. Without it you'd be stuck in bed, without it we'd both be stuck in bed."

"As long as we're not stuck in the same bed."

"Bleeding poofters!" another disembodied male voice shouted out.

"Arthur!" Gladys cautioned. "Leave it out."

"Yeah," Ronald replied with a broken-toothed grin.

"What happened to you?"

"Same as happened to you. Life happened."

"You know, I mean did you have an accident or a disease or what?"

"Bloody hell, where did you find this bloke, Gladys? No manners at all."

"You're a fine one to talk about manners, Ronald."

"Hey, Green."

"Bob."

"Hey, Bob. I guess you didn't know you can't go around asking people about their disabilities. Not done."

"That so."

"It sure ain't. So, what are you in for?"

"Funny guy."

"I try my best."

"Gillian Berry or something like that."

"Guillain-Barré? Wadda you know. Welcome to the club, Bob."

His club? Oh, but I am so screwed, I thought. So very, very screwed.

"You know the real kicker though, Bob? I was a bomb disposal engineer, me. Out in Iraq, Afghanistan. So, what happens? All those tours and not so much as a scratch.

When the bomb finally went off, it wasn't an IED or a mine, it was my own bleeding body exploding. Fancy that. What a bugger, huh?"

"You said it, man"

"And you? What did you do?"

"Clothing. Wholesale. Safer than bombs."

That's if you ignore the heavy duty takeover action.

"Yeah. So, Bob, tell me, how long you been out of hospital?"

"About seven, eight weeks."

"Let me take a wild guess. The MO said that function might come back with time or might not? Something like that anyway."

"Don't you dare, Ronald!"

"Haven't you ever heard the expression, Gladys, 'the truth shall make you free'?"

"John 8.31, Ronald. I know it well," she'd replied. "But, Christ's words are nothing but ashes in the mouths of nonbelievers."

"Excuse me," I'd interrupted. "I hate to get in the middle of this religious dispute, but, yes, that's more or less what the doctor told me."

"And that's what they told me too. Where I am now, is precisely where I was a month later, six months later and now, five years later."

"You mustn't mind what he says, Mr. Green. Each case is entirely different. Ronald's experience is Ronald's experience, not yours."

"What I am trying to tell our American friend, Gladys,

is to stop looking for John Wayne and the bloody cavalry to come riding up over the ridge, but to embrace his wheels and roll on with his life."

What kind of crappy life would that be, I wondered.

St. William

Rain sweeps across the covered market stalls, battering noisily against the colored awnings. People hunched beneath umbrellas rush by on Gentleman's Walk, a pedestrian street that runs along the bottom of the market.

"Winter has proper settled in," says the greengrocer, as he reaches over his boxes of vegetables to give me change.

"I guess so. Feels really cold today for the first time."

Water drips from the awnings and runs down the aisles to the open half pipes embedded in the concrete at the end of each row of stalls.

"That's the East Wind, that is. Ain't nothing to stop her between us and the Russian steppes, they says."

As long as it doesn't bring anything else Russian with it, I can probably survive the wind.

"She come in off the North Sea and cuts right through you, she do."

The English spend a lot of time talking about the weather as if it was a foreign invasion. Being an island, I suppose it is.

"Can't be much cop in that chair when it's like this," he says.

"No, not much fun at all. You mind putting the stuff in the rucksack for me?"

"No bother at all, sir," he says, coming out from behind his counter.

Wheeling a chair in Norwich isn't easy. The steep cobbled lanes and narrow streets, so quaint to my able-bodied American eyes, have become jolting nightmares. The outdoor market is built on Guildhall Hill which slopes down from the City Hall. I hardly noticed the slope when I was walking. Now it is almost all I do notice as, even with all my strength, it punishes my arms and my back. Being stuck in this chair has thrown me into another world, one littered with obstacles, blisters, a stiff neck and squeezed down to the essentials. It's a total, unending nightmare is what it is.

I wheel slowly to the bottom of the market, bumping carefully over the drainage pipes, squeezing past the stacked crates, children in buggies and other shoppers. I pause under the last stall, gathering myself for the 30-yard push through the rain to the covered Arcade. That's the first leg of a tedious journey to catch a bus in Castle Meadow. For the last part, which is up a very short but very steep hill, I'll have to ask someone for a push. I hate all that Blanche DuBois, depending-on-the-kindness-of-strangers crap.

"Have you been saved, brother?"

Standing in front of me is a thin, grinning, crazy-eyed character in a shabby dark suit and a clerical collar. He hands me a leaflet. Hesitating momentarily, I take it.

"Saved from what?"

"Have you been born again in Jesus, brother?"

"Not so I've noticed. So, no. Listen, I think…".

"Well, that's wonderful, because your time is now. This very day, if you come to Jesus and our holy Saint William, you will soon be able to cast aside your wheelchair and walk once more. I assume you want to walk again?"

"Ah, I suppose so."

"Excellent. Not like the others then."

"Others?"

"Many other unfortunates who I have tried to bring to Jesus and St. William. They refuse the gift that St. William can bring them. They have rejected him and they have mocked me."

"Morning, Mr. Motes," a voice behind me says.

"Detective Sergeant Richards."

I turn around. His plastic raincoat is pearled with raindrops, and long, wet strands of bald-man's hair are plastered across his forehead.

"You know what I'm going to say, don't you, Mr. Motes?"

"I am only wanting to bring him the gift of St. William's blessing, Detective Sergeant. No harm in that, is there?"

"Goodbye, Mr. Motes."

Reluctantly, Mr. Motes turns and walks off into the rain. He's carrying an umbrella, but doesn't open it.

"Thanks for that," I say. "Now I really am saved, saved from that religious lunatic."

"I was passing and saw you there being harangued."

"So, who was that guy? A priest?"

"He used to be. He was defrocked, or something

like that, for trying to revive a local saint, who for some reason, is no longer in favour with the church. Have had complaints that he harasses people, especially the disabled. So, we regularly have to move him along. Nothing serious. More of a nuisance. Terrible day?"

"Awful."

"Not what you'd be used to coming from California, I guess."

"Oh we get rain in California."

"Liquid sunshine. Isn't that what they call it?"

He is about thirty years out of date. I don't tell him.

"So, you keeping alright, Mr. Green?"

"Just fine, thanks. And you?"

"Can't complain, you know. How's that lovely little girl of yours?"

"Anna's good."

"And your wife, the local girl, she come back yet? That is if you don't mind me asking."

Cops can turn any conversation into an interrogation.

"Not yet."

"I'm sorry. Tough on the little girl that is."

"Listen," he continues. "I wondered whether it would be convenient for you to come up to Bethel Street and answer a few more questions."

"Now?"

"If it's convenient."

"And if it's not?"

"Then perhaps tomorrow."

"These questions would be about …?"

"The questions would be about the late Mr. Castle."

"Listen, Sergeant, of course I'm happy to help in any way I can, but why do you figure I can help? I didn't know the man and only spoke to him for a few minutes. He must have had friends or family who could tell you a whole lot more than I can."

"And we've spoken to them. Don't you worry about that. Like I said, Mr. Green, it's standard procedure is all it is. Tidying up loose ends, so to speak. And, of course, you were the last person we know of who actually spoke with the late Mr. Castle."

"I see. "

What I see is that Richards is taking far too much interest in me. I also see that if I don't cooperate he might take even more of an interest.

"I'll need a push up the hill," I say, slipping easily into Blanche, although I suppose Richards is not technically a stranger and most likely never heard of Tennessee Williams, a guy my dad never got tired of quoting given half a chance.

Little Sister

At first sight the row houses on Pilling Park Road appear to be all the same. Neat two-stories with small front yards. Look closer and you spot a liberating chaos. Mahogany-faced doors, stripped pine doors, doors with fanlights, new doors with or without glass panels, announce those people who bought their once city-owned houses. Doors painted institutional blue, the top half plain clouded glass, announce those who didn't.

Then there's the front yards. A ten-feet square of mown grass gives way across a picket fence to a sea of weeds and brambles. Regimented tulips look over a garden planted in broken-backed couches and rusting washing machines. A yard full of miniature windmills adjoins a patch of oil-stained cement.

Paddy Driscoll's front door, just like mine, is pale blue. His yard is motorcycles. Mainly Harleys and bits of Harleys. As the taxi pulls up I see Paddy sheltering from the rain in his doorway. He completely fills the space, his head brushing the top of the door, his bulk pressed against the sides. A post-apocalyptic barbarian; ear rings, face rings, rings on every finger, tattoos, head shaved except for a long ponytail. If my father could see our next-door neighbors, he wouldn't turn in his grave, he'd rotate at speed. But as native guides through the mysteries of surviving in England, Paddy and Molly have been our salvation.

"Hey, Greenie," he calls out as I am unloaded from the taxi. "You back a winner?"

"What?"

"The gee gees, mate."

"English, Paddy, talk to me in English."

"A horse, did you have a win."

"No. Why?"

"Taxi."

"OK. I get you. No such luck. The cops are paying for it."

He raises his eyebrows, but doesn't ask the next question.

Having so little money, taxis are out for me. Luckily, within a few level blocks of the house there is a ramped bus, when the driver can be bothered to drop it, that runs to and from the city.

"Someone come to see you."

"Yeah?"

Until the cops called I felt safely anonymous in my new life. I'd figured three countries and three passport changes was enough to put me and Anna out of sight. Now I'm not so sure. I've started to look closely at cars parked in our street.

"Who was it?" I ask, trying, without success, not to imagine a Russian hitter with a sniper scope drawing me into his crosshairs from behind a tree across the street in Lion Wood.

"Don't know, some woman."

I relax.

"I let her in. Don't mind, do you?"

"No, guess not."

"Ain't like you got anything to nick. Am I right?"

"Like always, Paddy."

She meets me as I came through the door, the words pouring out in a rush.

"I'm terribly sorry for imposing like this, I really am. The man next door, who I must say was very kind, you know, considering, said it would be alright if I waited inside, you know, because of the rain and everything and I just had to see you as soon as I could and…".

"Hold on, lady. Just hold on one second. I don't…".

"Oh, yes, of course you wouldn't, would you? How silly of me. I've been in such a flap since it happened."

"Happened?"

"Benjamin."

"Benjamin?"

"I'm Benjamin's sister, May, May Quest."

"Benjamin?"

"Yes, of course, you know, Castle, Benjamin Castle. He was my older brother, quite a bit older really."

"Right, I'm with you now. Listen, I'm sorry about your brother, Mrs. Quest, but I've told the police all I know, which isn't much at all."

"Do you mind if I sit down?" she asks.

I gesture to the chair. She perches.

May Quest is in her early thirties and tightly wrapped,

literally. Her blond hair is pulled back so hard it tilts her face up. It is a pretty face, even behind the librarian glasses. She wears a grey padded-shoulder suit, sensible shoes and hugs a tan Gucci handbag to her chest. They are the genuine articles. Expensive. She is well groomed and, by the sound of her vowels, apparently well educated. Totally the other side of the street from her late brother.

She opens the handbag and takes out a pack of cigarettes and a small silver lighter.

"OK if I smoke?"

I shrug.

"It's just that I've heard in California they're very strict about smoking."

"We're not in California right now."

"Of course not. Silly me."

"So, Mrs. Quest, what else do you know about me?"

"Oh nothing at all. Only what they told me down at the station."

"Gee, that's just swell."

I roll into the kitchen to get her an ashtray.

Not Waiting to Happen

"I don't care what the police say."

"Which was?"

"Well, of course, they wouldn't say it in so many words, you understand. There has to be a postmortem, an inquest and all that. But I know they think it was an accident. And once they get it into their heads it was an accident, well you know how it is."

"You don't think it was an accident?"

"You might not believe this, Mr. Green, but my brother was a very careful man. Extraordinarily careful in fact."

"I'm sorry to tell you this, Mrs. Quest, but the last time I saw him he was also extraordinarily drunk."

"He usually was. It was his legs, you see. Not having them, I mean."

She glances at my legs and then looks away hurriedly.

"But the drink never stopped him being careful. Never."

"Why not tell this to the police?"

"I did. I tried. They wouldn't really listen. They said as far as they could tell there hadn't been anything untoward, anything suspicious. Said I was just upset. Which I am, of course. He was my only brother, you see, besides my son, Harry, Ben was in fact my only blood relation."

"So why come to me?"

"I wanted to know what he said to you. His last words, at least assuming you were the last person he spoke to."

"You mean the cops told you all about me, where to find me and they didn't tell you what I told them?"

She flushes.

"It's somewhat complicated, Mr. Green."

"I can see that."

"It wasn't official, you see. As it happens, an old friend from London, haven't seen her for years, well, she works at the Bethel Street Police Station. I saw her there in the office. Such a small world, isn't it?"

"Oh, yes. And getting smaller by the minute."

"Please, you wouldn't tell, would you?"

"Tell who?"

"I don't know, the police?"

"No," I laugh. "I won't say a word to the police. You can count on it."

"Thank you ever so much, Mr. Green."

She pauses to light another cigarette.

I will have to air out the house before Anna gets back. My daughter is the real Californian when it comes to cigarettes. She was only four when she started giving chiding lectures to people she caught smoking in the street. Her crusade has not diminished with age, but then she is only five.

"And?" I say, trying to get things moving again.

"And? Oh, of course, yes, well, she found out your name and address for me."

"And that I'm from California?"

"She probably just heard that, station gossip I guess."

"Careless talk costs lives," I mutter.

"Pardon me?" she says with genuine alarm in her voice.

"Nothing. An old film I saw."

"Oh, I see. So that was all I had, your name and address. And that you were the last person to talk to him."

"More station gossip?"

She offers a nervous smile.

Yet again I recount the story of Legless Ben's drunken ramblings.

"I'm sorry about your brother, Mrs. Quest, but that's about all I can tell you."

"Oh dear," she says, putting her hand to her mouth. "Poor Benjamin."

She weeps silently. I stare at my feet.

"Forgive me, Mr. Green," she says after a few minutes. "It's been so difficult the last couple of days. Such a shock really."

A gust of wind rattles the front window. Although it is only two in the afternoon it's getting dark outside. Another storm coming in from Russia on the East Wind.

"I bet it has," I reply, trying my best to sound sympathetic, but failing to hit the right note.

She doesn't notice. Maybe she doesn't care.

Trust

I've always made it a point to stay well connected. When I started high school I cultivated the tough older kids who could protect me and teach me what I needed to know about being a tough guy, that is the extra stuff I could add to what I picked up from the guys who worked for the family. Then there were the ones who had phony IDs to get us booze on the weekends. I knew the smart kids, essential for homework, and the kids whose fathers ran useful places like the movie theatre, the deli or the video store. By holding all the strings without getting them tangled up I made sure everyone owed me favors. As a result other kids came to me with their problems. Then they too became part of my web. I was someone you could depend on, someone who you could trust, someone who always had an in. I was a fixer. If whatever it was couldn't be fixed friendly, then I could usually get together enough muscle to make it work.

"Bobby", my father said, "look at you, a regular throwback to Brooklyn. A modern person I wanted for you, and what do I get? A Louis Lepke? A Gurrah Shapiro? A Kid Twist?"

So, with that pedigree I was a natural for the family business which rested on connections, string pulling, trust, and a little judicious leaning or at least, and most of the time, the threat of leaning. It all worked until the Russians landed. They replaced trust with fear, leaning with broken bones and if that didn't work, with dead people. Then they replaced us.

All the strings now cut, disconnected for our own safety, I have washed up in Norwich, my only connection being tied to this cockamamie erector set on wheels. I am also more or less broke, for besides the light bulbs and the toilet paper, Tina has also made off with most of my cash. However, despite this change of fortune, May Quest must sense a glimmer of my previous incarnation.

"Mr. Green, I really don't feel right about all this."

"Meaning?"

"About what happened to my brother. I just know in here," she puts her hand over her heart, "that it wasn't an accident. I don't care what the police say."

"Having a feeling is OK, Mrs. Quest, but it's not going to cut much ice with the cops."

Her head falls.

"Any idea about who might want to harm your brother?"

"Well, maybe, but I don't really think I should say. That doesn't mean he wasn't, ah, you know."

" 'Course it doesn't. Did the police tell you if they found his wallet?"

"As a matter of fact they didn't. Why do you ask?"

"Well, if they found his wallet and the money was still there, chances are it wasn't a mugging which got out of hand. And from what they've told you, I would assume they did find his wallet and the money."

"I see. Yes. That does make sense."

"So unless you can think of someone who might be involved, I don't see where you could take this."

"What about that list he told you about, and him being the next one on it, and those other people who died?"

"The police had heard it all before. I suppose there were inquests as well. They don't seem to think there's anything to it. A figment of his imagination is what they said."

"Oh, Mr. Green, I just don't know what to do? I really don't."

"What about your friends, Mrs. Quest, or your sister-in-law? Can't they help out?"

"I'm afraid she and I don't get on at all. We never have. She was his helper, you see, his paid helper. From some agency I think. Do you have someone? An assistant is what they're called now, I think."

"No, this is only temporary for me. I manage by myself more or less."

"Well, Benjamin, he couldn't. He required help with certain personal things. I'm sure you understand what I mean. She was only working for him a couple of months when they got married. What did she want with a man old enough to be her father? That's what I asked myself."

I bet she had asked her brother the same question, probably adding "and in a wheelchair".

"I knew the answer too," she adds.

"Which was?"

"Money, Mr. Green. Prosaic, I know, but true. Of course, you couldn't tell Benjamin that. He was a very proud man. Very stubborn."

Legless Ben may have been proud, but he did not

appear to be wealthy, just the opposite in fact.

"You're telling me you think his wife could have dumped him in the river for his money?"

"Did I say that?"

"Not in so many words, but that seems to be your drift."

She crosses her legs and leans forward.

"Let's just say it's within the realm of possibilities."

She really doesn't like her sister-in-law.

"All my friends are in London, except for dear old Sally, the one I told you about. You see my family's not from Norwich, at least originally. I've only visited once or twice since my parents retired and moved up here."

"That's strange, your brother sounded more local than the locals."

"You mean the accent?"

"That's right."

"That was Benjamin blending in. Being one of the people as it were. He always wanted to be one of the people."

She makes it sound as if he had been trying to contract an unpleasant disease.

May Quest smoothes her already-smoothed skirt over her knees. She takes a deep breath and squares the shoulders of her well-tailored suit.

"Mr. Green, I simply must get back to London. Now I know it's expecting a lot, and, of course, you can say no if you want to, but I wondered if you would mind just asking around for me?"

"Asking who about what?"

"People about Benjamin. I want to know what really happened. What was going on. The police are obviously not going to find out. They've got their minds made up."

"Listen, Mrs. Quest. It's not really what I do".

"What exactly is it you do do, Mr. Green?"

"At the moment, not much of anything."

"Well then, it shouldn't be too difficult for you to find the time, should it? Besides, his friends may be more willing to talk to you, seeing as how you, well, you know what I mean."

I have a pretty good idea.

"Mrs. Quest, I don't know any of your brother's friends. I've only been in Norwich for a short time. I'm a foreigner. I wouldn't know where to begin."

"You could start with his widow. I'll give you her phone number."

"Mrs. …".

"Of course, I would be prepared to pay you for your time. Within reason, that is."

"Within reason," I repeat.

Presidential Duties

"Tell me again about the President and the animals, Daddy. Please."

"Come on, Anna, honey, it's time to go to bed now. School tomorrow."

"Please, please, please. Just once more time, Daddy."

"OK, I'll tell you then you go straight to bed. Is that a deal?"

She nods, sticking out her hand. We shake on it.

"Well, the President sent some men from the FBI to ask you and me to do very, very, very secret work for him. It's so secret that we can't tell a soul. Not our best friend, not our teacher, no one."

"And it's so, so secret," she says, repeating a story she knows by heart, "that we had to go on a big airplane and even had to change our last name."

"That's right, sweetheart. We had to change our name so nobody would know who we are or what we're doing."

It is the best time of the day. My child in her pajamas, sleepy and warm and trusting and in my lap. It is the worst time of the day. Betraying her trust with my story, telling her we will be seeing her mother very soon. What makes it so damn painful is she believes me. Why not? I'm her father and she's five. Chanting her favorite song, she never tires of reminding me of her trust and making me aware of my betrayal. 'You meant what you said and you said what you meant, my daddy is faithful, one hundred percent.'

"Go on, Daddy. The rest, please. Tell the rest."

"In Mexico City we found out that there were some animals in the zoo that were very unhappy. Remember?"

"Yes, especially the bears. They walked back and forth and back and forth. And the big monkey, he wasn't very happy either, was he?"

"That was a gorilla, sweetheart, and, no, he wasn't very happy at all."

"And when he finds out about all the animals who aren't happy, he's going to do something about it, isn't he? The President is."

"He certainly is. But we have to finish our special secret zoo report first. And we still have to visit the big zoo in London."

"And then we can go back home and see Mommy?"

"Then we can go home and see Mommy."

She puts her arms around my neck and squeezes tight.

"I love you, little girl."

"Love you too," she whispers, her head against my shoulder.

After a time she crawls off my lap and gets onto her mattress in the living room. I roll across and pull the duvet up under her chin.

"Not even Harley or Molly?"

"That's right, Pumpkin, not even Harley or Molly."

Clutching the teddy bear she calls BaBa, Anna puts

her thumb and part of the bear into her mouth and turns towards the wall. A few minutes later she is asleep. I sit watching her.

The last year had been a lot to ask from a five-year old. Does she really believe the story? Maybe she is too frightened not to believe it and that's why she sings her rendition of Horton at me and she asks for a rerun of our mission every night.

There is a crash from the back yard, followed by the rattle of tin cans. The crude alarm system I rigged up this afternoon has caught someone. I switch off the light and wheel over to the side of the door. Have they found me so soon? Everyone else seems to have. I pick up the old cricket bat I left there just in case, back the chair against the wall and lock the wheels. I've worked it all out. How to swing the heavy bat without sending the chair in the opposite direction. Where to aim. The knees. After that I'll have to improvise. If there are two of them I'm going to need more than improvisation. Quick switch hitting might be good.

"Hey!" Paddy yells "Get out of it!"

A muffled curse. More clanging of tin cans. The sound of heavy, urgent running. Kids screwing around. I relax. Paddy is a large step up from tin cans and string.

"Bleedin' eejits!" he shouts after them.

A door slams. Quiet. I put the bat back in the corner. Anna stirs on her mattress.

She is the worst thing about being stuck in this stinking wheelchair. If anything happened, how could I protect her? It isn't only the Russians that worry me. What if she hurts herself while playing in her room upstairs? Or in the back yard? What do other people in wheelchairs do? Helpers. That's it. Like Legless Ben. I don't want that. What I want is not to have to stick a tube up my dick to pee. What I want is my legs back. Two things it seems Bobby 'the Fixer' can't fix.

Point A

A few blocks from our house, Ketts Hill, a road hemmed in by rows of, what I've been told, are late Victorian houses, drops away in a long sweep towards the river and city. For most people it looks picturesque. From a wheelchair it looks like a bone-busting accident waiting to happen.

"You want to be getting yourself an umbrella, love," the old woman waiting with me at the bus stop says. "Catch your death."

"Maybe so, lady, but I can't push my wheelchair with one hand, can I?"

She looks down at me and then quickly away.

"Oh, I see, yes, how silly of me. I'm sorry, love."

I give her a damp smile. She stares across the road and fiddles with the large pink hydrangea on her head.

A bus pulls up, sending a wave of gutter water over my shoes. The door opens. Without a backward glance, Hydrangea Lady gets on.

"Sorry, mate," the driver says, "ramp don't work."

"What do you mean, it doesn't work? I can see it's a manual one. All you have to do to pull it up and drop it here on the sidewalk."

"That's all, is it? You know how much the bleeding thing weighs? Don't reckon you do. And you're asking me to bend over and lift it four times? Twice to get you on, twice to get you off. Well, I ain't about to do my bleeding back in, am I? Health and safety, mate. That's what it is. Health and safety. You should know all about that."

"I should?"

The door closes. He guns the bus, the back wheels smack into a puddle and my shoes are given another soaking. Nice guy.

Before I got wheelchair bound I'd never given much thought to getting around. There was always some simple way to get from point A to point B. Not any more.

I start to push myself home. I'm pretty strong, but it's raining more heavily and my plastic raincoat catches under my arms making it difficult to get leverage. My leather driving gloves are sodden. This is no fun at all.

A small white van pulls up and stops. It's Paddy.

"You want a lift there, Greenie?"

"Wouldn't say no. You going towards the city?"

"Can do if needs be."

He gets out, comes around to the passenger side and helps me slide in. Then he folds my chair and puts it in the back on top of the oil-covered motorcycle parts.

"I owe you one, Paddy."

"No problem, mate. What's neighbours for? Where you off to?"

"Bishops Bridge Road."

"Right you are. Just down the bottom by the river that is, across from Gas Hill."

He puts the van in gear.

"Who was messing around in the backyard last night?"

"Kids buggering about is all. Maybe on the lookout for something to nick. Sure gave 'em a scare with them tins and string."

"Oh that. Just something I put up for Anna and Harley to play around with."

"Yeah?"

I haven't shared my concerns about other possible visitors with Paddy. Until the cops started hitting on me I didn't think much about it.

Two minutes later we're there.

"How you getting back?" Paddy asks as he closes the van door.

"Maybe I'll get lucky and find a bus driver without a bad back."

"Well, if you don't, give me a bell. I'll be up at mine. You don't want to be waiting in the wet. Wouldn't take no time to nip down."

"That's good of you, Paddy, but I'll be OK."

"Yeah, well whatever, hard man. You know where I'm at if you needs me. Mind how you go now."

He drives off.

What should have been a ten-minute walk or a two-minute drive has taken me over an hour. This slow motion life is killing me.

New Widow

The Castles' place is in the middle of a row of solid, grey-brick three-story houses. The old stone bridge over the river at the end of the street is closed off to traffic which makes the whole area very quiet. Across the street, a round blue sign tells me, is the Great Hospital and that it was built in 1249. If this was California, the real estate guys and the developers would have already bulldozed and subdivided. I mean, who the hell needs a hospital that's so old, especially if there's money to be made?

I push the wheelchair-height bell. A few moments later Delia Castle opens the door.

This is not my idea of a new widow. Her drab shapelessness has vanished into tight jeans, a designer tee-shirt, my expert's eye says a genuine one, and no bra. She has a startling shape. Her hair shines. Her eyes shine. Her fingernails gleam a hard red. And she is smiling.

"Hello, Mr. Green. You're a bit late, aren't you?"

"Yeah, sorry about that. The bus was screwed up and …".

"Yes, well I know exactly what you mean. Not to worry. Come in out of the wet, please."

I push up the gently-sloped wooden ramp and into the hallway.

"Thanks for seeing me, Mrs. Castle. I know this must be a tough time for you."

"Well, it is, of course," she says, dimming the smile and

casting her eyes down. "But life goes on, doesn't it? Come through to the lounge, and I'll bring you a towel so you can dry off."

She pushes open a tall paneled white door. I wheel through.

The room is high ceilinged and furnished with antiques. The front window looks out on the street and the back, through an open-plan kitchen, gives a view onto a lush garden, an enormous grassy field and beyond that the high-spired Cathedral. There are gilt-framed paintings on the wall. Landscapes. Still lives. Old, murky portraits.

Even though his sister said he had money, from the look and sound of Legless Ben I had still expected a funky place, posters taped to the walls, cushions on the floor, candles in wine bottles.

She comes in and hands me a large, soft towel.

"Oh, that's great, thanks very much."

"Not a problem at all. Can I get you like a cup of tea, Mr. Green?"

"No thanks, I'm good."

She sits down opposite me on a long grey couch. I try not to look at her breasts, the nipples large and obvious through the tee shirt.

"Nice place," I say.

"Thank you. It belonged to Ben's parents. His father was a barrister, you know, what you Americans call a lawyer."

Next she'll be offering me glass beads.

"Right, thanks."

"They both died a few years ago. A car crash. A terrible business out on the Acle Straight. You know it?"

"Afraid not. I haven't been in Norwich all that long."

"A dead straight road between here and Great Yarmouth. Big ditches on either side. A lorry overtook coming the other way. No place to go really. Of course, that all happened before I met Ben."

"I see. How long ago was that? If you don't mind me asking."

She gives me a searching stare and taps her fingers on the arm of the couch. Her smile has turned brittle.

"That would be his sister, right?"

"What?"

"She's been on to you about me, hasn't she? Rubbishing me. Bloody interfering bitch!"

This is going well.

"Like I said on the phone, Mrs. Castle, Mrs. Quest asked me to talk to Ben's friends, that's all. Wanted to know more about the list he talked about. She thought you'd be able to give me some names."

"She's always resented me, you know. Right from the start. Ben didn't care though. He didn't like her much either. Said she was grasping and jealous. She and her husband are well off, but that didn't stop her from wanting all this too," she says, sweeping her arm in a circle. "She got a load of money, so it wasn't like unfair or anything like that. But the house went to Ben in the will and that really got up her nose. And now she must be really angrier than hell."

"Because it's yours?"

She gives me a tight grin.

"Because it's mine."

She stands up, goes to the front window and stares out into the street.

"May thinks someone killed him, doesn't she?" she says still with her back to me. "Pushed him in the river."

"More or less. Although she doesn't know."

"Of course," she says with venom, "she doesn't know. How could she?"

"Mrs. Quest thought perhaps it might have been the person who drew up that list he was talking about."

"List?" she laughs. "There is no bloody list, Mr. Green. Except in Ben's mind, that is, or rather that was."

She turns around. With the light behind her I can't see her face clearly.

"You know what she'd really like, don't you?"

"I think she only wants to know what happened to her brother."

"Ha!" she snorts. "Pigs might bloody fly."

She moves across and stands in front of me, hands on her hips. I have to arch my neck to look up at her. I hate that.

"May would like to think I was responsible. That I murdered my own husband. That's right, don't look so shocked. Then she'd have it all back, wouldn't she? House, paintings, furniture, the bloody lot."

"She never even hinted at anything like that, Mrs.

Castle, believe me."

"Oh, I can believe you, it's her that you can't believe."

"Well, listen, she only asked me to talk to some of his friends. That's all I'm going to do. So, you don't need to worry about what she might think."

"You obviously don't know my sister-in-law, Mr. Green."

I haven't even got to first base with this thing and already it's getting complicated.

She returns to the couch and drops down.

"Look, Mr. Green, you saw him at the pub, didn't you?"

"Sure."

"Well?"

"He'd had a lot to drink."

"No. He was drunk, Mr. Green. Drunk as hell, and as usual. I always told him it would happen one day. I warned him. But you saw what he was like. Never listened. Always knew best. I thought it would be a car though, not falling in the river. You see, he used to push out into traffic like a he owned the road. Said no one would run over a person in a wheelchair. Said they wouldn't dare. Poor Ben. My poor dear Ben."

She takes out a handkerchief and dabs at one dry eye and then the other.

Such grief is real tough to watch.

Defeating Death

"I told him, if you're so wrapped up in all these damn disability things, why didn't you marry a disabled person? At least she might be as interested in it all as you are."

"You weren't?"

"I wasn't not interested, it's just that I wasn't nearly as interested. How could I be? Why should I be? He was always going on about bloody able-bodied people this and bloody able-bodied people that, although he said 'temporarily able-bodied people'. He'd just got there before the rest of us was how he saw it. Then it was all about how they didn't understand, how they discriminated against disabled people, how they patronised disabled people, and here I am, Mr. Green, and what the bloody hell am I?"

I nod, trying to look like I know what she's kvetching about.

"I'm bloody they, that's what I am! Jesus! It's all very well to go on and on about how terrible we are, but where the hell would you people be without us? Sorry, didn't mean you, of course. Don't know anything about you, do I?"

It is two in the afternoon and she started fixing herself large martinis about an hour ago, explaining that while she didn't usually drink at this time she was sure I would understand, especially as Americans knew all about martinis. She's on her third or fourth and not bothering with the olives.

"Sometimes I think he didn't want a wife, just a cheap live-in skivvy. It's not easy, Mr. Green, not easy at all. All the attention focused on him. You know what I mean? All the attention. All the time. The poor disabled person. The brave disabled person. The important disabled person. And there's me doing everything for him - cleaning, cooking, shopping, helping him in and out of bed, helping him bathe, helping him dress, helping him on the loo, helping him when he falls out of his chair and all the time I was invisible. Not there was where I was. He even told me that, said that I shouldn't say anything if I went to a meeting with him. 'Disabled people must bloody well speak for themselves'. That's what Ben used to say. Disabled people must speak for themselves. Bugger that! Let him cook for himself then and make the damn beds and clean up his own mess in the bathroom, pick himself up off the bloody floor."

She throws back the rest of her drink and plunks the glass down hard on the coffee table. Then she gets up, walks over to sit in a leather easy chair closer to me. Leaning forward, the top of her tee shirt billows open. I pull my eyes away only to find her staring at me staring at her. I'm trapped. She knows it and gives me a slow tipsy smile. Is this what happened to Legless Ben? I grip the wheels of the chair and ease myself backwards.

"Please don't misunderstand me, I loved Ben dearly, it was only that sometimes… You sure I can't get you a drink? No one likes to drink alone."

"Thanks, but it's a bit early for me."

"Me too," she says, with a rough laugh. "But, I'm

making an exception today. An exception in memory of Ben, my late husband, Benjamin H. Castle. I can do that, don't you think?"

"Sure thing, Mrs. Castle. "

"Delia."

"Delia."

She stands up, giving me a booze-hazy look. She moves across and past me. Suddenly I feel her hands on my shoulders, pressing lightly.

"You know what I am going to miss, Mr. Green," she whispers into my ear.

"Bob," I manage to squeak.

"You know what I'm really going to miss, Bob?"

"What's that?"

She tightens her grip.

"You guess. Go on, guess."

"I'm not what you might call a real good guesser."

"Doing it," she giggles, "on the wheelchair."

I haven't even thought of trying to push that button since my legs stopped carrying me around and my waterworks demanded piped assistance. I didn't imagine that people in wheelchairs could go there.

"Right. You know something, Delia…".

She spins the chair around expertly. She's leaning over me, her hands gripping the sides of my chair, her face a few inches from mine. Slowly she begins to push me towards the far wall of the room.

The chair stops moving. Still holding it with one hand

68

she reaches up and undoes the top button of her jeans.

"You know what I do know, Bob?"

I shake my head.

Her jeans are on the floor.

"I know how to defeat death," she says, pulling her tee shirt over her head.

"How's that?"

"Fuck for life," she says.

Sounds pretty reasonable to me. Better than that, it apparently sounds more than pretty reasonable to my too-long-hibernated cock. I glance down. Spring has definitely sprung.

Old McDonald

" I'm really sorry, sweetheart. Please stop crying now. Come on."

"You promised! You promised! Crossed your heart and hoped to die, you did."

"Anna, please. I told you…".

"Promised, promised, promised!"

The promise - solemn, binding, a constant emotional anchor for a little girl, in a strange house in a strange country, far away from her mother and her friends and on special assignment for the President of the United States to save the animals – was that I would always be there when she got out of school, either in the playground or waiting at home. This is the first time I've missed.

I hold out my arms to her. She refuses to budge. She stares at the floor. Her arms are held tightly across her chest. Molly stands by the door with Harley, looking on. I am powerless with guilt.

I've felt this way since my cell phone rang about half an hour ago, with the ring tone Anna had insisted I set – "Old McDonald Had A Farm". At the time I was entwined with Delia Castle on my wheelchair, feeling immensely relieved and immensely pleased, stupidly pleased with myself. The doctor told me that I might require Viagra. Apparently not. I had experienced my very own, non-chemically-aided resurrection! Things were definitely looking up. That is until Old McDonald.

"Don't answer it," Delia said, her head lolling on my shoulder.

She reeked of gin and vermouth.

"Sorry, but I've got to."

"Bob, Bob, Bob, don't you remember?"

"Remember?"

"Remember death, Bob. You can't defeat Mr. Death so quickly."

She stuck her tongue into my ear. Old McDonald kept bleeping from the back of my chair.

"I've really got to, it's probably about my daughter."

She'd sat up sharply.

"Your daughter?"

I managed to free one arm and reach around for my rucksack. As I did, Delia got off me, picked up her clothes and strode out of the room.

It was Molly on the phone. She told me that I had a very upset daughter.

"I'm sorry about this, Molly. I really am."

She said that I should save my 'sorry' for Anna. Personally she didn't give a toss where I was or what I was doing. If I wanted to be a thoughtless wanker, I should do it on my own time, not hers or my kid's. That made me feel a whole lot better.

Delia came back fully dressed and flopped into the easy chair. She looked dazed.

"I gotta be going. It's my daughter you see."

"Oh, how very very nice for you."

I couldn't read whether she meant it, but then she was pretty drunk.

"Yeah, she's five."

"Ah, bless. You got a wife to make up the set?"

"An ex, back home."

"Long way, back home."

"Sure is."

She stood up, holding on to the back of the easy chair and swayed slightly. I started for the door.

"Thanks for the names and phone numbers. I'll give you a call."

"You do that, Bob. You come by any time you want. After all I've got all the facilities here for you, don't I? Everything fully, one-hundred percent accessible."

I wondered whether that included her.

"Would you like to have a look? You haven't used the loo, have you? Or seen Ben's stairlift. You really do need to see Ben's stairlift, Bob. Good old Ben's stairlift."

"Maybe some other time, thanks. I'm running late."

"You really do need to see it," she sobbed. "You really do, Ben's bloody, bloody stairlift."

Weeping, she sagged against the door frame. I leaned back in the chair, as I went down the ramp and into the street. Paddy was waiting beside his van.

Honor thy Father

It's cloudy, but at least it's not raining for the first time in days. Paddy is sitting on top of the four-foot-high brick wall which separates our back yards. He's kicking his heels like an overgrown kid. I'm resetting the tin-can alarm system.

"You got yourself a problem here, Greenie?"

"No, not really."

"So why the trip wires?"

"Wadda you mean trip wires? I told you before, it's just something for the kids to play with."

"Greenie, I ain't the sharpest knife in the drawer, but I bloody well know trip wires when I sees them."

"Is that right."

"Sure is."

He takes off his leather jacket and rolls up his shirt sleeve.

"See this one here?" he says putting his finger on one tattoo among a tangle of tattoos.

I roll over to get a closer look. It's difficult to make it out.

"My first one. I was but seventeen. Legio Patria Nostra. Honneur Fidelite," he reads.

"OK, I'll bite."

"The Legion, Greenie."

"The Foreign Legion? Desert forts and funny hats?"

"And the rest of it. It was my old man what was to blame. Used to knock my mum around something terrible when he'd had a few. One night I stopped him. Knocked the old bastard spark out. Banged his head on the sink. Way my mother carried on, I figured I must have killed him. He was laying there stretched out bleeding like a stuck pig all over the kitchen floor, my mum screaming at me for a murderer, what the hell else could I do?"

"I can think of a few things short of joining the Foreign Legion, Paddy."

He puts on his jacket, pushes himself off the wall, drops to the ground and comes over near me.

"Well, you're an educated man, Greenie. I was just a dumb Mick traveller who'd killed his father. By the time I found out he weren't dead, I was over there and already enlisted. The Legion ain't really understanding about things like changing your mind."

"How long were you in?"

He squats and pushes at the tin cans.

"Long enough to know this ain't for no kids. We set these out when we was on patrol. You been in the service, Greenie?"

"No, too young for Nam and then they scrapped the draft, which was fine by me."

"All this carry-on, a heavy-duty bolt on the front door, new window locks. What all that in aid of, mate?"

"I don't think you want to know, Paddy. I really don't."

Still on his haunches he suddenly grabs both wheels of my chair and gives me a hard stare. Then very slowly he begins to tip me backwards. I flail my arms, a turtle about to be flipped over.

"Hey man! Paddy come on!"

He doesn't let go. I stop trying to resist.

"Who you after kidding, boy?" he asks, lowering the chair gently, all the time holding my eyes.

"OK, OK, you made your point. But I don't intend to let anyone get that close."

"What anyone would that be?"

"The who is safer not to know, believe me."

"You reckon if I didn't know who it was, you'd be safer?"

"Hey, Paddy, don't twist my words around like that. You know what I mean."

"Is that so? Now let's say this here 'anyone' come around to do you some damage, right, and I hear you and the kid shouting and screaming or whatever, and what you is telling me is that you want me to stay out of it, just keep watching East Enders? That how it's going to be, Greenie?"

What's to do?

I tell him about the Russians. All the time I'm talking he's crouching in front of me, locked on to my eyes, his 'Love-Jesus' tattooed hands resting on my wheels.

"Blow me!" he says standing up. "You're a dark one, mate. Here we're thinking we got us a nice quiet Yank moved in next door. Family man too. Oh no, what we got us is a Jew gangster on the run. How about that."

"Yeah, how about that. But listen, Paddy, I'm no

gangster. Sure, what we did was not legal, but there were no guns, no cement overshoes, none of that heavy, sleeping-with-the-fishes stuff. Which all maybe explains why the Russians found us so easy."

"You saying your lot got too soft?"

"Something like that, yeah."

"Thinking on it now, you've never sounded much like a gangster, to be honest, unlike those Sopranos, always effing and blinding like they do, I've never heard you swear, I mean like actually swear, like using the f-word. Blaspheme yes, heard too much of that from you, but then they even do that on the BBC, along with the rest of it."

"That's my dad. When I was a kid I swore like trucker, never in front of him though, but after he passed, I don't know, it didn't seem right anymore. Not that I don't want to at times, not that I can't help myself at times. Then there was Anna and I didn't…".

"Yeah, we feel the same way about Harley."

He reaches down and pats my knee. The bonding of the non-swearers. I'll take it.

"So, Greenie, you think they're going to find out where you're at?"

I shrug.

"It's possible. But no more than that. Just have to be real careful."

He holds one of the strings and gives it a tug. The tins jump and rattle. A little night music.

"Yeah, real careful, Greenie. Maybe you need yourself some real protection."

"Meaning?"

"You know."

"I do?"

He makes his fingers into a pistol and picks off an unsuspecting sparrow perched on the roof.

"Ain't that how it goes with you people?"

"What do you mean, 'you people'? Come on, man, I've already explained all that."

"Well, whatever. You want something, I know people who could get it. Just give me a shout."

"Christ, you been seeing too many of those dumb movies, Paddy."

"From what you say about the Russians, maybe you ain't been seeing enough of them. And I don't think our Lord has nothing to do with it."

I choke my laugh into a cough.

"Yeah, Paddy. You're dead right about that. Jesus Christ has nothing to do with it, nothing at all."

Every Cloud

Death always comes at the right time for somebody. Legless Ben's midnight swim is turning out that way for me. I was down to my last few twenty-pound notes and trying to believe that something would turn up to add a little to the disability payment I get, thanks to the social worker at the hospital. Now it has. £500 plus expenses is not much, but maybe it will do until I can get out of this wheelchair and find a real job. Until then I figure having to drag my sorry ass around Norwich talking to cripples and looking over my shoulder for nosey cops and revenge-bent Russians.

Paddy has dropped me at a day centre for handicapped people in the middle of the city. 'The Norwich Inclusion Centre' it says over the front door. It is a rambling one-storey, prefabricated, permanent temporary building. The windows are dirty. The yellow paint is peeling. Inside there is a wide and worn-down linoleum-floored corridor with open-plan rooms coming off of it. Despite the prominent no smoking signs, the place smells of cigarettes, together with boiled tea and disinfectant, the latter which doesn't quite mask the odor seeping out from two wide doors marked "Toilets".

Two old men in wheelchairs nod at me as I roll in through the automatic doors. I return the greeting, pretending to be in on their secret.

Brendan Connor is the first one on Delia Castle's list, and he looks like a dictionary definition of 'cripple'.

Slumped sideways in a large electric wheelchair, his body, arms and legs and face are tensed and twisted and, of course, there are drool lines down the front of his purple sweater.

He rotates his head and bright blue eyes measure me. Grimacing, he lets fly a staccato volley of noise.

I smile in what I hope is an appropriate way and look for help to the tall, powerfully built young black guy who stands behind his chair.

"Brendan says you must miss California on a day like this."

Brendan's entire body curls in on itself and shakes. The black guy laughs, which I suppose means Brendan is laughing. I force a laugh, just to show what a good sport I am.

"Say, how the hell does he know where I'm from?"

"Don't ask me, man. You gotta ask Brendan yourself."

Now no one is laughing.

I'm not getting the hang of this at all. I turn to Brendan.

"Right, Brendan. How did you figure out about California ?"

His head jerks to one side and he mutters something.

"Pretty obvious, he says."

"It is?"

Brendan grunts, splutters and then swivel-head gurns at me.

"Yeah," his friend says with a snorted laugh. "Right enough you are, man. Right enough. Brendan, also says not to worry, you'll get used to that chair. Takes time that's all."

What's it with this smartass cripple? How'd be figure all that out? Castle's wife. Yeah. Sure, got to be. No magic. No mystery. Still and all, this crazy spastic bastard is creeping me out big time. Need to plough on and then get my sorry ass out of here.

"Look, Brendan, the name's Bob Green and like I told your friend here on the phone, I got your name from Delia Castle, you know, Ben Castle's wife…".

I'm interrupted by another set of grunts and random body movements.

"Brendan says, of course he knows Ben's wife and knows that his sister has hired you to talk to his mates."

This is totally nuts. Always two steps ahead of me.

Brendan's body goes very still. He stares at me with what appears to be pity.

Being wheelchair bound might have got me through the door, but it's not getting me very far with Brendan.

"Hey, Brendan," calls out a fat young man who lurches past on elbow crutches. "You alright there, boy?"

Brendan says something and the fat boy laughs. What I've got here is the village comedian. If only I could get the damn jokes.

I explain that Ben's sister doesn't think the drowning was an accident.

"Did he ever say anything to you about some kind of a list, Brendan?"

He draws a bead on me. Angry? Frightened? Can't tell.

"Ben also said something to me about some other handicapped people...".

Brendan jerks and splutters.

"Disabled people!" his companion says with passion. "Disabled people!"

"Whatever," I reply.

"No what-ever," Brendan says, twitching spastically in my direction. "Dis-abled."

"OK, man, I'm sorry. Lighten up. I'm new around here. Right? Disabled people. OK? He mentioned Sarah and Janice and somebody else I can't remember."

"Bar-ry," Brendan says. "Bar-ry."

"That's right, Barry."

"Dead", he says.

"That's what he said. Then about the list. Can you tell me anything about that?"

He shakes his head and spits out something to his friend.

"Brendan says he has to go now," the other says.

"Right, OK, but can you tell me anything about how those people died?"

Brendan ignores me, swings his wheelchair away and rolls off towards the end of the corridor near the automatic doors. As he does a gang of about half a dozen young kids in blue and white school uniforms, maybe 10 or 12 years old, rush through the entrance and talking loudly and gesturing, they surround his chair. It looks as if he is under attack, but his companion seems totally cool about it. He tousles a couple of the kids' heads and laughs. They all disappear around a corner.

I start to follow when a tall thin man steps in front of me. He's carrying a freshly-minted salesman's smile.

"Good morning," he says, sticking out a hand.

"Hi there," I reply, shaking his hand.

"I'm David Yallop, the deputy director."

"Bob Green."

"Hi, Bob, nice to see you. It's your first time with us, isn't it?"

"What?"

"First time at the Centre. Social Service usually tell us when we've got someone new, but you know how they are. Paper work gets lost and…".

"Oh, no, no, I'm not coming here, like them, I mean, not coming here."

"Like them?"

"The people who come here. You know. Nothing like that. I came over here to talk to somebody, that's all. "

"Oh, I see," he says, the welcome-to-camp look fading.

"Like them?" he muses.

"I mean, it looks like a real nice place you've got here."

"You think so?"

"Yeah. Sure is. A real nice place, like I said."

He doesn't look convinced. Why should he. It's a total dump.

"Well, we do the best we can."

Brendan's helper comes out and gestures to Yallop.

"Excuse me for just a minute will you, Bob."

I flap an 'OK'.

A guy in Stevie Wonder shades and attached to a German Shepherd glides toward me. I start to move backwards, but the dog takes him smoothly around my chair. A few yards away three old women slumped in wheelchairs are sneaking looks at me. Outside the front door a small white bus is disgorging a troop of people in various stages of stumble, roll and dribble. I need to get out of here before someone pins a note with my name on me.

"Mr. Green?"

"Yeah?"

Yallop's lost my first name. Not good. The salesman smile has been replaced by a sour expression which looks much more at home on his bony skull.

"Henry tells me you were asking Brendan questions about some of his friends. Is that right?"

"Yeah. Is there a problem?"

"Not a problem as such. However, as you can imagine, it's been an upsetting time recently for all of us, and you've upset Brendan pretty badly. That's not the kind of thing we want for our people here at the Centre."

"Hey listen, man. I'm sorry about that, but I was only…".

He holds up his hand while shaking his head slowly. The smell of disinfectant and toilets comes back. It's been there all the time but now seems more aggressive.

"I'm afraid I am going to have to ask you to leave now,

Mr. Green. Duty of care, you understand."

I don't, but leaving suits me just fine.

I force my chair past the incoming gaggle of cripples and out into the clean cold morning.

A Bird in the Hand

"Hey, mate. Over here, over here."

I can't see anyone, just a thin, high-pitched voice coming from a thick screen of bushes at the side of the building. Cautiously, I roll towards the sound.

"That's right, come a little further, mate, a little further."

Around the far end of the Centre, against a brick wall, sits a little hunchback guy in a miniature electric wheelchair. Black hair combed straight back, skimpy Zapata moustache, a leather jacket covered in studs and wearing shades despite the overcast skies.

"Keep coming. Come on, come on so they can't see us."

"So who can't see us?"

No answer. His small hand scoops at the air between us until we are alone behind the bushes, facing each other wheel to wheel. Soles of tiny motorcycle boots brush my knees.

"What's the problem, buddy?" I ask.

He stares at me, then cackles high and raspy.

"Buddy," he says in a painful American accent and then laughs again. "What's the problem, buddy!"

Candy wrappers are laced in the bushes, the dirt under us obscured by crushed cigarette butts. My fingers are numb with the cold.

"I'm freezing my ass off, so come on, man, cut the crap and tell me what's on your mind."

"OK, me old china, don't get your knickers in a twist. Ben Castle is what's on my mind," he says, the laughter gone.

"How's that?"

"I hear you've been asking."

"You heard that from Brendan?"

"I'm not saying from who. Just heard, that's all."

"You knew Castle?"

"Sure. All of them, mate. Knew all of them. Barry, Janice, Sarah and now poor old Ben. Knew 'em all, I did. Mates they were. Bloody good mates."

"So why are we hiding out here? Why couldn't you tell me this inside."

"Ain't safe, mate."

"What do you mean it ain't safe?"

He looks around, swinging deaths-head earrings. Then he leans forward and grips my forearm. His small many-ringed fingers dig sharp through the thick fabric of my jacket.

"They gets to know if you says something they don't like. Sure as tomorrow they does. They got spies or the place is bugged with microphones and that. Can't be too bloody careful, you can't."

"Who's 'they'?"

He shrugs, the leather lifting at a hard angle off his crooked shoulders.

"Yallop?" I venture.

"No, it ain't Yallop. Anyways, I don't think it's Yallop.

You think it might be Yallop?"

"How the hell should I know. I just got off the boat, for Christ sake."

He mangles a smile.

"I guess you did and all. 'Off the bloody boat.' I like that."

"If not Yallop, then who?"

"Someone else. Some wanker has it in for us and that's for damn sure."

"That's not very helpful, is it? I mean if it's not Yallop then it has to be someone else. Right?"

"You ain't listening too good are you, Yank?"

"The list? You're telling me there really is a list of ...?"

"No idea, mate. Ben thought that one up. Said it stood to reason there had to be a list with all them accidents one after another like there was. Sure, Ben thought that up about a list, made a fuss about it too and look where that's got him. Another bloody accident, right?"

"Well, that's what the police figure, an accident, but maybe you should wait for the inquest."

"Inquest? Inquest my arse!" he spits. "Everyone knows about inquests and disabled people. We're nothing but accidents waiting to happen, ain't we? Fact of the matter is we're accidents that have already happened. Inquest! Inquest? Might as well wait for the second bloody coming."

This guy sounds as crazy as Castle. Maybe they're all nuts.

A cell phone blares out the theme tune from 2001. He

claws at his jacket pocket.

"Bugger!"

A small silvery fish pops out of his hand, flips slowly end over end as if sailing into outer space and falls to the ground, escaping under the bushes, still ringing its insane jingle jangle over and over. From under the arm of his wheelchair he grabs a short stick with a rubber tip and tries to pull it towards him. The phone burrows deeper into the candy wrappers and butts. The ringing seems to be getting louder.

"Oh shit!" he squeaks, dropping his stick.

"I'll get it," I say, pushing my chair near to the bushes.

I lean as far over as I can, but the phone is out of reach. The ringing is incessant, crowding all other sound from our hidden space and spilling into the world beyond. Then that world is upon us.

"Everything alright here, Martin?"

Over the top of the bushes looms David Yallop's gloomy horse face. I'm a teenager caught smoking behind the gym.

"Phone," Martin manages to say, pointing at the bushes.

Yallop steps around, ignoring me and snags the phone. As he picks it up the ringing stops. He pats off the dirt. Then he retrieves Martin's stick. He doesn't return it or the phone.

"There. Seem to have missed your call. Too bad. I hope it wasn't important. I'll clean it up for you in a minute. Don't you think it would be better to come into the warm now?"

"Good idea," Martin replies.

Without a word to me he does a swift 180 and heads off with Yallop following a couple of shepherding paces behind, taping the stick against the side of his leg.

Time to get the hell out of here.

Catching The Bus

Paddy said he would meet me at the Forum, the city library, when I was finished at the Centre.

"Don't figure you for a reader, Paddy," I had said incautiously.

There was a three-beat silence.

"A knuckle scraper, is that it, Greenie?" he replied finally and without anger. "All grease and grunts?"

"Hey, man, I'm sorry, didn't mean it how it came out."

Paddy's the last person I want spitting in my soup.

"In actual fact, you ain't far wrong," he said, as the van swung into the Kett's Hill roundabout, "Last one I read all the way through like, besides the Bible of course, was that American one about Zen and motorcycles. Too much Zen, too much scenery, not enough motorcycles."

"I never got into that."

"Zen or motorcycles?"

I looked across. He was smiling broadly.

"OK, Paddy, you win."

"Right," he laughed, "I'm just going down there to use the computers, Greenie. Looking to find me some parts, crossover pipes, glide yokes, spacers, you know what I mean?"

"Can't say that I do. You know, motorcycles are not really my thing."

He turned to me.

"Fair enough, mate. Fair enough. By the way, Greenie, what is your 'thing'? What lights your fire?"

A simple question, but for a long moment I couldn't remember when I had a life which held anything more than learning to be a full-time father while surviving as a crippled foreigner hiding in an English backwater. Enough to be getting on with. My taken-for-granted LA life - the family business, the one I assumed would always be there, weekend surfing, weekend fathering, jazz at the Catalina Bar and Grill, at Charlie O's, Blues at McCabe's dinners with friends at La Vecchia on Main Street, all that belonged to someone else, to the walking, almost-legit Bobby Fishbaum.

"I guess I don't have one right now, Paddy," I answered finally. "A thing, I mean. Working on the day-to-day just about fills her up."

"Well, maybe you needs to be working on something else. Take you out of that day-to-day. Now if you wasn't a Jewish person, I'd be after bringing you over to our church."

"Like you say, Paddy, I am a Jewish person, so thanks, but I'll take a pass on that invitation."

I am thinking once again about what Paddy said and thinking about my former life and what was coming, as I push myself away from the handicapped centre. When all this started it was going to be a long vacation for me and Anna. Sure, that's all, and when it was over we'd be able to go back home, settle in and pick up the threads. Yeah, right. From the get-go I knew that wasn't going to happen. This is no vacation, there is no way back. Never has been. This is it, this or some place like it.

I need to get my head straight with how it is and maybe with this dumb-ass wheelchair too. What next? Like Brendan or Martin, under the thumb of a Yallop? No way. I lean forward and bear down as hard as I can, pushing at the wheels again and again until my forearms burn.

You can get across the ring road from Vauxhall Street to Chapelfield Gardens, a small park near the middle of the city, by using an underpass. It works swell, especially if you go for the smell of piss. Instead, I wheel over to the pedestrian lights and wait with two old ladies in cloth coats and old-ladies' hats. A couple of aged chickens, they cluck, cluck, cluck at each other and nod their heads fervently. We're joined by a group of uniformed school kids and a few other people. They crowd behind us.

A heavy stream of traffic is coming from the right. Fast and purposeful, drivers trying to get through the lights before they change. "Oh Mary", I hear, a thick whisper so close its warm breath kisses my ear. Then an unexpected heaviness on the back of my chair, a shove and I am rolling, weightless into the metal flow. I grab for the wheels and lean back as hard as I can. Too late! Dead meat rolling! Brakes scream, the old ladies scream, the kids scream, I scream. A bus, three times bus size, fills up the space above me. Every detail is etched. The light rain sparkle on large bus window, the black wipers, the pink and blue stripes, the blue wheelchair symbol, the driver's eye-widened face. I wait for my life to flash in front of me. A blank screen. No reruns, no movie today. I am about to die without reflections.

A jolting thump on my right shoulder and I am going over, flying in the air, a rag doll. My body hits the ground again and slides and slides. No pain now. Tire squeal washes over me, car-crash-broken-glass sounds from a distance, road sandpaper grating my face, metal rice crispies snap-pop-scrunch.

Silence.

"Jesus!" someone shouts.

"You OK, mate?" calls another.

"Someone ring 999."

"Lie there right still, boy."

I'm surrounded by lots of sports shoes.

I lift my head a few inches off the road. A yard away under the bus is the skeleton of a porcupine. Damn things get everywhere. At least it's not a dead skunk. No, it's, it's my wheelchair! My mother-jumping wheelchair!

No! No! No! It took me weeks of battling with the public service people to get a comfortable one light enough to push without killing myself. All over again, I'll have to start all over again. God in heaven!

Too much. Too damn much. I give up.

Slowly I let my head drop down on to the road and close my eyes.

Accidents Happen

"There you are," says the blond male nurse, as he finishes the last stitch in my forehead. "As good as new. Almost anyway."

"Thanks."

"You know, you're one lucky bloke. Walking away from an accident like that. Oh, yeah, well, sorry, you know what I mean."

"Sure, I know. Don't sweat it."

I'm learning my job as a crippled person - putting other people at ease.

And here I am at my ease, lying on a padded table in the emergency room. Even though they've given me a shot, my body hurts everywhere, including places I'd never heard from before. Nothing broken, lots of scrapes and bruises.

"You lay there real still, boy," the ambulance guy had told me. "You're gonna be just fine."

"Your bicycle ain't doing too good though," his partner said, bending down to look under the bus.

Messed up as I was I couldn't help laughing. It hurt.

Then lots of questions from the doctor in the emergency room, less about the accident, more about why I can't walk.

Now there's a uniformed cop standing over me. Young, red cheeks, no helmet and a notebook. More questions.

"Am I prepared to take what?"

"A breathalyzer test."

"You're not serious."

"It's standard procedure, sir."

"Drunk in charge of a wheelchair? Is that it?"

He doesn't answer.

"If you wouldn't mind blowing into this tube, sir."

"Listen now, officer."

"Constable."

"Yeah, OK, Constable. You going to listen or what? I hadn't been drinking. For Christ sake it's not even lunchtime. I was pushed off the sidewalk right in front of the bus."

"First things first, sir."

That seems pretty 'first' to me, but his policeman's dance has been choreographed. He's not letting go.

He holds out something which looks like a calculator with a plastic tube sticking up at a right angle from the base.

"It's new," he explains. "Digital."

"Yeah, wonderful. I just love digital."

"Sir?"

What's the point. With some difficulty I prop myself on one elbow and blow into the tube. I sink back. He checks the readout and writes down the result.

"That's fine, thank you, sir. Now you allege you were pushed off the pavement into the path of the oncoming bus?"

"Right. Pushed."

"I see", he says, writing in his notebook. "Did you manage to see who did this pushing?"

"How the hell could I, he was behind me. There was a crowd of people. I just felt it, that's all. Felt the push."

"You're positive about that, sir?"

Did I imagine it? No. I can still feel the burst of acceleration as the chair took off, feel the whisperer's breath. "Oh, Mary." A homicidal priest with a grudge against cripples? Unlikely. Cripples and priests are a too perfect match. So if not the Catholics, who? The same person who sent Ben for a midnight swim? How did I get on that list so quickly? Asking too many questions maybe. What about the Russians? Could be. No, not so quickly. Jesus! Got to call Paddy. Got to get Anna out of school. Got to… Got to calm down is what I've got to do. Right down. Get rid of this cop and then get the hell out of here. How am I going to do that without a wheelchair? Give me strength!

"The curb slopes quite sharply just there", says the policeman, intruding on my panic. "Are you sure your wheelchair didn't just accidentally move and then sort of take off down the slope? I mean, no one came forward at the scene, although, of course, if you insist that you were pushed, we can go back and take further statements, get CID involved."

"CID?"

"Criminal Investigation Division, detectives. If we move from a road traffic incident to a serious crime such as attempted murder…".

That kind of involvement I most definitely do not need.

"Well," I reply hurriedly. "Now that you mention it, the slope that is, I guess someone could have bumped into me maybe and then before I realized it I was down there in the traffic. Makes more sense, wouldn't it? After all, who'd want to off a guy in a wheelchair?"

"If you're sure, sir, absolutely sure. I mean to say that if you really feel someone was attempting to harm you…".

"Hey, no, I don't… I'm a little shook up is all. Dumb accident is what it was. They happen, right? Can we leave it at that? After all I don't even have any broken bones, do I? So how serious is that?"

Now I'm asking him questions. Mistake. He's giving me the policemen's stare.

"Well, in any case we will be reviewing the video footage from the CCTV cameras near the crossing. If there was anything untoward occurring we'll be able to spot it, don't you worry now."

Worry? This cop doesn't know from worry. Worry is another visit from Richards, more layers peeled away by more questions until Robert Fishbaum pops up, a jack-in-the-box target.

Eggs, Chips and Peas

"Everything's good, Greenie, just chill. Anna's next door at ours, she's fine."

"No one been looking for me? No one hanging around?"

"No, mate. You expecting visitors."

"Not exactly, but I didn't dive into the traffic, Paddy. I was pushed."

"Pushed? Sure about that?"

"You sound like the cop who came to question me at the hospital."

"Right," he says, giving me a narrow-lipped smile. "Can't be having that, can we?"

"Hope to hell not. Something else. Just before I felt the push a voice whispered 'Oh Mary' in my ear, or what sounded like that. Whoever it was had a foreign accent. At least I think it was a foreign accent."

"What kind of an accent? Russian?"

"Can't say for sure. Maybe. But leaving aside the $64000 Question of how they tracked me down, what the hell is a Russian doing whispering 'Oh Mary' before he shoves me in front of a bus?"

Paddy shakes his head.

"The thing is though," I say, "from what I've heard, they don't do 'accidents', they do like public announcements."

"You wanna translate that for me, Greenie?"

"Sure. Accidents can be accidents. You know, shit that just happens. Nothing to cause a ripple. Now a bullet in the head or a knife in the back or a car blown all to hell, that is a public announcement. Scares people. Discourages others from even thinking about messing with them."

"Gotcha. So being run down by a bus would not be...".

"Yeah, no announcement there, especially as the guy that was squashed was not Bobby Fishbaum, a guy who ratted them out to the cops, but some dude no one had ever heard of, a civilian so to speak."

"So, Greenie, if not the Russians, who would want to kill you?"

I shrug. It hurts when I shrug. It hurts when I don't shrug. I pop a couple of painkillers they gave me at the hospital and swallow them dry. Tough guy. Next thing I'll be eating my cornflakes without milk.

"Don't have a clue. Might be the same folks that sent Legless Ben for a swim. Like I told you, he was going on about someone murdering cripples. Said there was a list and he was next. Then his sister gives me some bread to ask around, talk to his friends, the crippled ones."

I tell Paddy about what happened at the handicapped centre.

"Sounds like you might be on to something, Greenie. You say these disabled guys were really scared?"

"Shit scared, I'd say. But besides Castle's widow, no one knows I've been asking about Ben and his list. That makes it hard to believe someone could arrange for me to catch that bus so soon after I'd been at the centre."

"Unless someone was following you," Paddy says.

"There is that. Damn! I have enough to worry about with the Russians, without having some nutcase cripple killer after my sorry ass as well. And here is me stuck in this piece of total junk," I say, banging my fist on the hard metal side of my Red Cross issue wheelchair.

"Christ on a crutch!" I shout, as the pain knives into my already banged up hand. I should maybe stick to dry pill swallowing.

"Not real clever," Paddy says, casting a critical eye, either over my wheelchair or me punching it, but more likely my blaspheming.

Must be more careful.

On a smooth flat surface I could just about manage to inch this clunky beast along, but outside, no way. Protecting Anna and myself would be difficult enough, but now I really am a sitting duck, a painfully slow rolling duck.

"I might be able to sort something for that, Greenie. Temporary like, until you get kitted out proper again. I know this bloke owes me a favour. You might also want to think again about the other thing we talked about."

"What was that?" I ask.

"You know," he replies, picking me off with a loaded finger.

"Let's not make things more complicated."

"Up to you, mate. Right, better get on to it. I'll catch you later."

He leaves and after a couple of minutes in comes

Molly and the two kids. Anna is holding tight to Molly's hand and looking at me with frightened eyes. That's not surprising. One side of my road-grated face is covered in iodine and I am festooned with bandages, over both eyes, the top of both hands and the back of my head.

"It's OK, baby. Daddy's had a little accident, that's all. Come on now, Pumpkin, don't cry."

Walking slowly, her head turned away, she crosses the room towards me. Still looking away, thumb and BaBa firmly in her mouth, Anna climbs into my lap and puts her head on my chest. I can feel her body shuddering with quiet sobs.

"You gonna be OK?" asks Molly.

"Yeah, nothing broken, nothing except the damn wheelchair."

"You'll have to be more careful, Greenie."

"Right. I'll do that," I say, not wanting to worry Anna by telling Molly what happened.

"You guys come over for your tea this evening. Egg, chips and peas, that be OK?"

I ruffle Anna's dark hair.

"Egg and fries, Pumpkin?"

I feel her nodding her head.

"Chips', Anna mutters into my sweater. "It's called chips."

"Sorry, baby. Of course it is. Chips. That's great. Thanks Molly. Thanks a million."

Press On

"**P**lease, Mr. Green, it wouldn't take but a minute or two. A few minutes and a couple of photos is all we need."

She is standing at the bottom of the wooden ramp that lets me roll up and into the house. A three-quarter-length Burberry trench coat over a stylishly plain grey jersey dress, Prada ankle boots and a leather tote bag. Even from six feet, I can see these are not knockoffs. She's wearing at least $4000. Not what I would expect with a low-level reporter working for a local rag. What other kind would be sent to interview a crippled accident victim on a council estate?

"Mr. Green?"

Miss $4000 is tall, thin and coffee latte. Late 20s at a guess. Rich black hair worn long, a broad forehead, wide-apart hazel eyes and a nose that has been broken and badly set, a flaw, together with the raised scar over one eye, that only serve to make her perfectly beautiful.

"Mr. Green, can we come in out of the rain?"

"Yeah, sure. Sorry. Come on in."

She and a young guy with a bulky bag over his shoulder come up the ramp. As soon as the door closes behind them, he begins to unpack a camera.

"Hey now, pal. I didn't say I was going to let you take any pictures. You want to holster that camera?"

He hesitates and looks over at the woman. She nods

and reluctantly he puts the camera back in his bag.

"It makes a much better story if we had a photo, Mr. Green. More of the human interest angle, especially as everyone could see how badly injured you are."

Right, and with all newspapers going out on the Web, maybe someone, somewhere, somehow recognizes Mr. Green, 'an American rundown by a bus', as Bobby Fishbaum who was, and then maybe they yak to someone, somewhere and somehow that finds its way back to the Russians and then for sure I'm screwed. That is if the bastards haven't already found me.

"Sorry, Miss ...".

"Garanday, Annabel Garanday," she says, handing me a business card. "And this is Andy, our photographer."

Apparently, English photographers don't have last names.

He nods at me unsmiling, uninterested. I return the favor.

"You see, Miss Garanday, I'd rather skip the pictures if it's all the same to you." Which I know it isn't. "My daughter has been upset enough already by what has happened, and a picture in the newspaper, well, would only, you know, just kinda stir it all up again and make it worse for her. I want her to forget all about this."

"In my experience, Mr. Green, children just love to have their photo or their parents' photo in the paper. They show their little friends and...".

"You have kids, Miss Garanday?"

"It's Ms and no, I don't have children, but...".

"So we're good with no pictures? Yeah?"

She replies with a resigned smile that says we're not good.

"Will you at least be prepared to answer a few questions?"

"Sure thing. What do you want to know?"

She reaches into her tote and pulls out a shorthand pad and a pen.

"Well, let's start with the accident, shall we? Tell me what you remember."

I tell her, leaving out the 'Oh Mary' bit.

"I see," she says. "But what about you being pushed off the pavement?"

"I'm sorry. Where did you hear that from?"

She looks confused, off balance.

"Didn't you tell the police someone pushed you."

"There must be some kinda of misunderstanding here, Ms. Garanday. Anyway, who told you that I was pushed?"

"I'm afraid I can't tell you that, Mr. Green."

"I see. Sorry to disappoint you then, but it was all my fault. You see, I'm new to this wheelchair thing. I must have slipped, pushed forward when I should have pushed back, that's all. A dumb-ass accident. No big thing. For sure not anything that will be interesting for you or the people who read your paper."

" 'A slow news day', isn't that an American expression, Mr. Green?" she laughs, but not with her eyes. "Here in Norwich almost every day is a slow news day. So, a disabled American almost killed...".

"Slow down now. Just slow right down. I'm not in the hospital. I'm not on a life support machine. Nothing is broken. Do I look like I've been almost killed?"

"Journalistic license then."

'Underworld Figure dies in Valley Rest Home'. 'Russian Mafia Indicted in Phony Rag Trade War'. I already have had more than enough journalistic license in my life.

"OK, Mr. Green, I can see the accident has unsettled you. I understand that. At least you could tell me about how you came to live here in Norwich, where you come from in the States. You know, interesting background that I can use."

Better I should paint a target on my face.

"I'd really love to help you out Ms Garanday, but I've told you what happened and now I've got to go pick up my daughter from her school. So, if you will both excuse me."

Annabel Garanday shoves her notebook into her tote. Photographer Andy hoists his bag onto his shoulder. She is clearly pissed off. He is clearly bored.

I wheel to the door and open it. Outside the rain is falling more fiercely. Bracing themselves, the two step gingerly down the slippery ramp and onto the sidewalk. I close the door.

Copped Out

"**M**y daddy is doing in the toilet right now. You'll have to wait there."

Anna is talking to someone at the front door and, as she says, I am 'doing' on the john. With two dead legs it is not easy moving on and off the seat or dealing with my pants. I have to lift each leg with my hand, bend over and rock back and forth to work the underwear and then pants legs up or down and then transfer across to or from the wheelchair. Luckily, Paddy got me a chair that's not all that different from the one I parked under the bus, so I don't have to make too much of an adjustment. Still, it takes about ten minutes to pull up and transfer over.

"He says he's going to the library, but he's just being silly."

She's a lot sharper than I was at her age. My dad used to tell me the same story, and I didn't figure out he was not really going to the library until I was nine or ten.

"Have you come from the President?"

I can't hear a reply.

I wheel out to see Anna at the door talking to Detective Sergeant Richards. He's wearing a sheepskin coat and a small-brimmed hat.

"Can I come in, Mr. Green?"

I wave him in. He steps inside and removes the hat.

"More about Ben Castle?" I ask.

"No, Mr. Green. I've come to talk to you about your

accident the other day."

Jesus H! When do the vultures stop picking at my bones? It's like you can't catch a bus - OK I admit, not the safest way to catch a bus, but it wasn't like I had options - without everyone landing on your doorstep looking for scraps.

He pulls a green folder from a thin document case and plucks out an official-looking paper.

"It says here that you told the police constable that you were pushed in front...".

I hold up my hand for him to stop and flick my eyes at Anna.

"Sweetheart, can you go over to Harley's house and see if he wants to play? Daddy has some business to talk over with Mr. Richards."

"Business?" she asks, looking from me to him. "What kinda business?"

"Grownup business. You know, just boring old stuff."

She sneaks another look at Richards. She's not convinced. With reluctant slowness she makes her way to the back door and goes out.

"I apologise, Mr. Green, I didn't realise the little girl didn't know what happened."

"She knows what happened. An accident is what happened. I told her and I told the police officer. I don't want her upset by having to listen to it all again. It's bad enough for her to see me like this."

Richard's grunts softly and looks down at the paper in his hand.

"It says here you claimed when first asked, that you were pushed, and then you said you weren't pushed. Did he get that wrong?"

"Nope. He got it right. I was upset. In a lot of pain. Mixed up. Angry. I guess I wanted to blame someone else for what went down. I mean, who wants to look like such a jerk? Then I figured being as how I was talking to the cops and it was official and all that I'd better get it right."

"I see," says Richards, glancing over at me and then down at the report. "Funny thing is, Mr. Green, that when we reviewed the CCTV footage, there wasn't any CCTV footage."

"And that means exactly what?"

"Usually nothing. Cameras break down, computers go wrong. We know that. This time, however, it was rather different. The camera stopped working about two minutes before your accident. The techs say it was caused by some kind of radio signal interference."

"So?"

"So, they can't figure out how it happened or why they started to get the feed coming back fifteen minutes later."

"Come on, you trying to tell me someone screwed with the camera on purpose, just so they could push me under a bus without being seen?"

Richards shrugged.

"Could be," he says. "If you hadn't given a conflicting account of what happened, well we'd have most likely put the camera malfunction down to gremlins, but this," he waves the form at me, "makes us think there might be something else more serious going on."

Wonderful. 'Oh Mary' is apparently all tooled up like a character from Mission Impossible. What am I thinking? This is totally nuts.

"I'm afraid I can't help you out, Sergeant. Like I said, it was a stupid accident. Nothing sinister. Believe me, if I really thought someone had tried to shove me under a bus, I'd be knocking on your door straight away."

"Of course you would, Mr. Green. I just wanted to double check, to make sure you're not in any danger."

"Danger?" I laugh. "Why in God's name should I be in danger? I haven't been in Norwich long enough to make those kind of enemies. Besides, you can't believe someone would go to all the trouble of messing with a surveillance camera just to get at me? Even if there was such a person, how the Sam Hill would they know I was going to be at that crossing at that moment? It doesn't add up, Sergeant."

He studies me with his weary detective eyes. I try to look suitably bemused.

"Your missing wife?" he asks hopefully.

"Tina? Do me a favor. That woman needed an instruction manual to change a lightbulb."

Although she did manage to unscrew them all quite handily. Maybe she found that manual.

He smiles thinly. Taking out a small notepad, he jots something down.

"I'm sorry to have bothered you, Mr. Green," he says,

putting the note pad away and returning the form to the green folder.

"No bother at all. I appreciate your concern. Thanks."

"Just doing my job."

He sticks out his hand. I take it. He puts on his hat, throws me a goodbye nod and leaves.

Hedgy

Hedgy is wearing a paint-spattered smock, a stiff blond wig, bright red lipstick and a five-o'clock shadow. He's a tall, thin guy with trembling hands. I might be mistaken, but it looks like he's wearing a yarmulke, as well as a large yellow flower over each ear. Hard to guess his age through all the makeup. Maybe mid to late sixties. When I had asked him over the phone whether Hedgy was his first name or last name, he told me it didn't matter as he had only one name.

"Like Rembrandt or Michelangelo," he said.

Sure. I can really get with his parents not giving him a first name. Of course, maybe that is his first name. Also, by the look of the paintings on the walls, even with only one name, I reckon that the lovely Hedgy ain't no Rembrandt or Michelangelo.

His studio is in an old brick warehouse on Oak Street. I am met at the door by a six-foot tall tailor's dummy in a trench coat topped by a rubber pig's head. The pig is grinning and has a fat cigar stuffed in its mouth.

Inside is a cavernous room maybe 70 feet by 50 feet, with skylights in the roof. The two shorter walls are closely hung with paintings and sketches. More canvases are stacked against the other walls. Two easels with empty canvases sit in the centre of the room and hanging from the roof beams are an old motorcycle with tires coming out at right angles to the frame and a number of headless tailors' dummies pierced with swords, knives and one impaled on a feathered spear. Three small windows look out on the building's car park. Opposite, a floor to ceiling picture window gives a view over a river confined on either side by concrete embankments. It would be picturesque if not for the rubber tires, a shopping cart, pieces of wood and other random junk that floats on or protrudes from the scum-green water.

"Welcome to my little world," Hedgy says, taking in his studio with a sweep of a broad and hairy hand.

"Yeah, thanks."

"Could you please look at me when you speak," he says, pointing to his flower-bedecked ears. "I'm deafened, you see. These hearing aids help a bit, but I still have to lipread to catch what you're saying."

And here was me thinking he'd just escaped from an Hawaiian luau.

Being from Southern California, transvestites are no big deal, but I'd never expected to run into one, especially a deaf Jewish one, if that is really a yarmulke riding on top of his Marilyn wig, in a place like Norwich. Then maybe everywhere is becoming like Los Angeles, without the weather.

In the far corner of the room there's a high tower made of twisted metal rods and pieces of odd-shaped plastic. I roll across to get a better view. I now see that the tower is made of dismembered wheelchairs. Next to it is an intact fire-engine red wheelchair on its own. In the seat is a portrait of a nude woman with flowing brown hair sitting in a wheelchair. She's strikingly beautiful. She's smiling.

Seeing my interest, Hedgy explains with a deep sigh,

"My Sarah. My muse."

I then notice that almost all the paintings are of the same woman at various ages and all of her in the nude and in a wheelchair. In one picture Hedgy is standing next to her. She's wearing a white wedding dress, so is he.

"Since she died," he says, "I simply cannot paint. My muse is dead, my heart is dead, my vision has flown."

"I'm sorry for your loss."

"So very American," he laughs, giving a coquettish toss of the head.

The wig shifts precariously to one side. The yarmulke stays put. Pinned to the wig I guess or resting on his hearing aids. I try, but can't pull my eyes away.

"Isn't that what your policemen say? Or is that just those on the telly who speak like that?"

"No, I think that's how they talk, but, of course, I don't have much personal experience with the police."

In fact, that's exactly what the cops said who dropped by the house after my dad passed. I like to think they meant it too.

Hedgy walks over to one of the front windows and looks out.

"Why didn't you bring your friend in with you? He looks interesting."

I had told Paddy he could split after he dropped me off. I figured I was having enough trouble getting through to Ben's friends without turning up with an extra from Mad Max. Now I'm here, I reckon Paddy would fit right in.

"You got stuff to do, man," I said. "I'll be OK. Give me

an hour or so. If you're not back by the time I'm ready to leave, I'll wait for you in that pub across the road."

"If it's all the same to you, think I'll hang on out here, Greenie. You don't seem to be all that clever with that new wheelchair I blagged for you. Last time I left you off to chat with a disabled bloke, they had to bring you home in an ambulance. We don't want little Anna to have her dad coming back covered in more bandages or maybe not coming back at all, do we?"

"Oh, he's fine outside," I say to Hedgy. "He's got calls to make."

"Right. If you're sure. Cup of tea?"

"No thanks, but if you have coffee...".

"Of course. Instant OK?"

"That will be fine, thanks."

The coffee is not fine. It's thin and tasteless. If I had really wanted decent coffee I could have gone to Starbucks, which, to my surprise, they have in the city centre, along with lots of other American fast food joints. Soft imperialism I've heard it called. So what, I like their coffee. It reminds me of home.

"Oh, yes, Ben and Sarah and Janice were like this," says Hedgy, showing me three fingers pressed together. "And, of course, Barry too. Called themselves, 'the Rolling Dervishes'. They had Martin and Brendan and, I think maybe a few others as well. The way things are going around here, soon they'll be a bloody endangered species."

"That's sort of what I've come to ask about."

He arches a penciled-in eyebrow at me.

"Well," I go on, "his sister, Ben's sister that is, doesn't think his death was an accident and then there's the list he was talking about and your ah, your...".

"Wife," he says with emphasis.

"Yeah, your wife and a few other handicapped people that Ben mentioned ...".

"Handicapped? Oh dear, Mr. Green. Oh dear."

Twisted-up Brendan too had gone apeshit when I said 'handicapped'. I figured that it was a step up from 'crippled', but apparently not.

"Another American expression?" asks Hedgy, lifting up his hands to centre the wig.

"I suppose so."

"Well, if you are going to visit more of Ben Castle's friends and don't want to put them off, I would advise you to use the term 'disabled people'."

"Right."

"You don't really get it, do you?"

"Ah, not really. We got 'handicapped parking', so I figured...".

"I'm afraid it's just like Shaw said, isn't it?"

"Shaw?"

"George Bernard Shaw. I assume you've heard of George Bernard Shaw?"

They might have lost their empire and become total crap at everything else, but the Brits have a way of putting you down that is second to none.

"Of course, that Shaw," I say, nodding as if I knew what the hell is talking about. "Disabled people it is."

Murderer He Wrote

"She was a student of mine at the Art School. Some years ago now. Life drawing class. First day the model doesn't show up, and this striking girl in a wheelchair volunteers to take her place. They didn't say anything, but you could tell the other students were terribly shocked. I mean, who had ever heard of a nude disabled model? She didn't turn a hair. Like she'd done it all her life. Just rolled over, popped herself across onto the chair and took her clothes off. That was it for me. I had found who I had been looking for all my bloody life and didn't know I'd been looking. I mean that. You know, it's been eighteen months to the day. Eighteen months. Jesus, but I miss her."

Tears streak Hedgy's mascara down his checks.

"You must excuse me. I haven't spoken so much about Sarah since the murder."

"Murder? I thought it was an accident."

"Semantics," he replies. "The police said it was an accident. The newspapers said it was accident, a horrendous accident is what they wrote. I say it was murder."

Finally, an answer.

"That's exactly what the police have said happened to your friend Ben. An accident they said."

Hedgy threw up his hands.

"They would, wouldn't they just. You see, in this case,

I know who killed my Sarah."

"Did you tell the police?"

"Oh yes, I told them in no uncertain terms."

"The newspapers?"

"Them too."

"And?"

"They were very polite about it, but they, the newspaper people that is, they insisted it had been an accident and it would open me to ridicule if they printed what I told them."

"The police?"

"The police said there was no case to answer."

"I don't understand. If you told them who you thought...".

"Know, Mr. Green. Not thought. Know."

"OK. If you told them who you knew the murderer was, why didn't they follow it up?"

"They didn't follow it up because they said I was crazy. Of course, they didn't come out and say 'crazy' just like that. What they actually said was that I was suffering 'grief-induced delusions'."

"I see. So, who killed your wife, Mr. Hedgy?"

"No 'mister', just Hedgy, if you don't mind."

"Right you are. Hedgy."

"You really want to know who killed her? Do you want to know the unspeakable thing that killed my Sarah?"

His voice rises an hysterical octave or two. His mascara-smudged eyes are now looking inside at the turmoil of his heartbreak.

"Sure. That would be great. But you know, listen, I am having a hard time understanding what you're telling me here."

"Perhaps if I introduce you to the murderer, you will better understand. Come over here."

He leads me to the other side of the studio. He points to a pile of small grey wheels, scraps of torn leather, pieces of metal tubes and smashed-up electric motors and circuit boards all scattered over a large red scrawl on the floor that reads 'MURDERER.'

"Would you credit it? A brand new machine. Cost £20,000. Climbs stairs, seat goes up and down, lets you stand upright. Does everything but make the bloody tea. Gyroscopes. Computer operated. 'Foolproof', was what the salesman said. His very words. Guess what? It wasn't even close to being foolproof. I demanded that they let me keep it as part of the out-of-court settlement."

"Settlement?"

"Oh yes indeed. My solicitor told me I should take them to court or hold out for more money, but I did not want to get into a long, dragged out affair and, after all, £850,000 is a lot of money, although I'd give every penny and more to have her back."

"It must have been some hell of an accident to do this."

"No accident did this. I did this. I call it 'vigilante art'."

"You junked £20,000?"

"Yes, £20,000. Unlike you people, we don't have

capital punishment in this country. However, in this case I made an exception."

"Hold up a minute. You telling me you executed a wheelchair?"

"Don't look so surprised, Mr. Green," he said, his eyes returning from their recent trip to pin me down.

I thought I was being accepting and cool about the Jewish tranny schtick and all the other weird shit going down, but Hedgy is definitely not playing with a full deck. I hate like hell to admit it, but the cops nailed this one pretty good. Calling him 'crazy' is an understatement.

"I can see you don't believe me. Fine. But tell me what else would you call a machine that crushes it's victim, breaks her arms, breaks her legs, breaks her neck. That's what this bastard thing did to my Sarah."

We look down on the remains of the killer wheelchair. He is weeping.

Internal Rabbis

"Listen, Hedgy, would you like me to go now? I seem to have stirred things up for you."

He shakes his head and then blows his substantial nose in a monogrammed handkerchief.

"I'm sorry, Mr. Green."

"Bob."

"I'm sorry, Bob. I mustn't go on so. Sarah wouldn't approve. You see, she was a fighter, not a moaner. Hated moaners, she did. Often said that too many disabled people spent too much effort moaning rather than getting out there and making things happen, making changes. Quite a woman was my Sarah."

"I bet."

Hedgy stares into the middle distance. The tragic artist, albeit now a very rich tragic artist.

"So, could you tell me what happened to Janice and Barry? Ben's wife was pretty upset when I saw her and only gave me numbers for you and a twisted-up guy in a fancy electric wheelchair I met up at that centre place. Had a big black guy helping him."

"That would be Brendan and Henry, of course. Maybe Morris."

"Didn't catch the black guy's name. But Brendan, that's right, Brendan. He wasn't very forthcoming. Actually, if anything, he was hostile. Don't think he wanted to talk to me."

"Yes, I expect maybe he wouldn't."

"Any idea why?"

"No, not exactly, except with Ben's death on top of what happened to the others, he must be upset, frightened even. Fact is, since Sarah's funeral I haven't seen much of those people. I do see Brendan, of course. Almost every day. He lives a few doors up the road. But disability stuff was really Sarah's thing, you see. Didn't want me hanging around too much with them. She was always saying that disabled people needed to take control of their own lives."

"I see. Ben's wife told me he said the same thing. But aren't you disabled, what with being a deaf person and all?"

He cocks his head to one side and smiles ruefully.

"Oh no, Bob," he laughs. "I am not even considered genuinely deaf by the bloody deaf community. You see, up until five years ago I was a normal hearing person, 'one of them', as deaf people might say."

That might be stretching 'normal' to breaking point, but then what the hell do I know about the ins and outs of this freaky handicapped world I've been tossed into.

"Then I became ill and lost virtually all my hearing. Never got on with learning to sign. Too old maybe. So here I am, neither a real deaf person nor a real disabled person. But at least I am tolerated by most of the deaf and by Brendan and the others too. Maybe because of being with my Sarah. Do you understand?"

I don't, but not wanting to keep the incomprehension tango spinning, I nod sagely as if I did.

"Do you know what happened to the other people who died?"

"Of course I do. Sarah told me. Went with her to the funerals as well. Janice who was the first one to pass away. Suffered the most bizarre mishap. Apparently, she was going down Earlham Road when the ground literally opened up and swallowed her and her chair. Right out of some kind of macabre Hammer horror film. I know, it sounds farfetched, but it seems that part of the city is riddled with old underground chalk workings. They'd been demolishing a building nearby and all the coming and going of heavy equipment, and knocking down of walls weakened the ground beneath the pavement. She used a rather substantial wheelchair. Had to really. You see, she was a quite a large woman, over 20 stone or something like that. Anyway she was terribly unlucky. Poor Janice, never had a chance. Took the fire brigade hours to recover her body, and, of course, her wheelchair."

"Jesus! That doesn't sound like anything a person could have done deliberately."

"Deliberately? Who said anything about 'deliberately?'"

"Ben's list. Remember? I started to tell you that Ben thought that handi... disabled people were on some kind of a hit list. Said if I wasn't careful I'd be on the list. Then there's his sister, who doesn't want to accept the police's idea that it was an accident. She's really why I'm here talking to you."

"Didn't know Ben had a sister. He never mentioned one or perhaps I simply didn't hear him talk about her. I'm afraid I can't be of much help about lists and that kind of thing, Bob."

"Did Janice have any relatives in the city? Anyone I could talk to about what happened?"

"I just finished telling you what happened."

"Yeah, I know, but I need to follow it up a bit more. Although from what you say, I don't see how it could not have been accidental."

"Well, let's see, there's her partner, Sylvia. She lives in the block of high-rise flats near the Centre where you saw Brendan."

"Sylvia?"

"That's what I said. A problem?"

"No, no problem at all. Just wanted to make sure."

"Don't have her number. Brendan's probably got it."

"Thanks, I'll see about that. And Barry, the other one who died?"

"Another strange accident, that was. Some kind of insulin thing got Barry. There was some misunderstanding with the district nurses who came in to help him out of bed in the morning and give him his injection. They said he had called to tell them he was going away. They must have got crossed lines somewhere. Then to make matters worse, his community alarm was on the blink as well, so when he fell out of bed he couldn't alert anyone. Poor bugger lay there a couple of days before they found him. Very upsetting it all was."

"One more accident then?"

"Apparently so."

"Family?"

"Wales."

"What?"

"Barry was from Wales, you know, the country."

Bastard!

"Got yah, Wales."

"They came over for the funeral. Suppose they went home afterwards."

"Accidents. Lots of accidents. You reckon what happened to Ben was another accident?"

"Not for me to say, Bob. After all, disabled people are quite prone to accidents, aren't they? Sarah would have told me off for saying that. She thought the non-disabled world, as she called it, was essentially set up to exclude her and the others, so that so-called accidents that happened to disabled people were not really accidents at all. They were what happened to them when they had the audacity to venture out."

"That sounds more or less what this little dude in a wheelchair was telling me."

"That would be Martin. Yes?"

"Yeah, black leather and cowboys boots?"

"That's him. Another Roller and a total pain in the bum. Sometimes I think that crazed dwarf really lives in another dimension, if you know what I mean."

Again, I smile and nod. In fact I don't have a clue what he means, as I can't imagine what 'another dimension' would look like to this crazy schmuck.

"And all this conspiracy stuffs sounds pretty nutty to

me as well," I say. "I mean shit happens, doesn't it?"

"I suppose it does at that. Can I assume then that all those cuts and bruises were self inflicted, or do we put it under the label of 'shit happened'."

Caught me again. Fucking Brits!

I smile. He smiles back.

As I get to the door, Manpig's trench coat flaps open - Hedgy must have flipped a switch - and inside I see half a dozen black-coated plasticine figures, their little arms twitching while raised imploringly to the heavens.

"I call this piece 'My Internal Rabbis'," Hedgy says with pride. "Always in there, always arguing."

I decide not to wait around for a fuller explanation.

Really Sorry

"**G**ood to see you again, Mr. Green. Please over there."

I wheel to a spot on the patient's side of his desk. At least he didn't ask me to have a seat, but then he sees a lot of handicapped people.

"I see here," he says, reading from the folder on his desk, "that you had a rather serious accident recently. Bruising, abrasions. Ah, yes, I can see your hand and a bad scrape on the side of your face. Seems to be healing nicely though. Otherwise, how are we?"

"We're still not walking, Doctor. We, meaning me, I am still having to use the catheters."

"Of course. I mean otherwise, Mr. Green. Everything else still in working order?"

"Far as I can tell, yeah."

"Well, that's very good to hear. Now, Mr. Green, you are, of course, quite free to say no, but if you don't mind I would like to ask three of our fifth-year medical students to sit in on our consultation today. As I informed you at our last meeting, your condition is quite unusual, and so it would be extremely helpful for them to see you and then afterwards have Dr. Ho discuss the diagnosis with them."

How do you say 'no' to that?

"Very good of you, Mr. Green. Nurse, please."

She goes out and almost immediately returns with Dr.

Ho and two white-coated girls and one white-coated boy. All three are wearing dangling stethoscopes, carrying clipboards and looking suitably bad-news serious. Dr. Ho, on the other hand, has no stethoscope, no clipboard and greets me with a big smile. He's apparently bad-news happy. Why not, with me the old bastard has found the Mother Lode.

"Now," says the doctor, "we would like you to ask Mr. Green some questions and then offer a preliminary diagnosis for us, one you might use to determine the bloods and other tests he might require. Please, Louise, if you'd like to begin?"

The taller of the girls steps forward. She's thin and homely and exudes equal measures of confidence and indifference. Perfect doctor material there.

"Good afternoon, Mr. Green. Would you please tell me why you find it necessary to be in a wheelchair?"

She makes it sound as if it were a lifestyle choice.

"I can't walk."

"I see. Could you try to be a little more specific for me?"

"How much more specific can I be, sweetheart?"

She appears momentarily off balance.

"Ah, yes. More specific. OK. So, let's go back to before you were admitted. Can you describe your symptoms? By that I mean how you were feeling."

"Thanks a bunch, but I do know what 'symptoms' means."

"Of course you do. And so…?"

I give her a minimalist rundown. She and the other white coats bend their heads and write on their clipboards. Dr. Ho continues to smile. My doctor remains expressionless.

"And when you were admitted to the ward, what happened then?"

Once again I give her the Readers-Digest version.

"Do you have any sensation in your legs at all now, Mr. Green."

"Some."

I am beginning to enjoy this game.

Louise reaches into the side pocket of her white coat and takes out a little stainless steel hammer with a triangular rubber head. She comes over to me.

"May I? Thank you."

She lifts one of my legs so they are crossed and then taps me somewhere below the knee. My leg jerks very slightly.

"Hyporeflexia," she comments, holding out the hammer to the others.

One after another they step across and hammer my knee. I am beginning not to enjoy this game.

The other students ask more questions. They write on their clipboards. They confer in whispers.

"Now," my doctor asks, "what are we looking at? Of course, you don't have any of the test results, but from what he's told you... Yes, Louise?"

"We all agree that what we have is undoubtedly a classic case of Guillain-Barré Syndrome. We base this on progressive shutdown of motor functions and the degree of subsequent recovery he's experienced. We also feel that he has been extremely fortunate to have regained so much in such a short space of time."

"Dr. Ho?"

Dr. Ho, now grinning with delight, comes and stands beside me and, resting his delicate hand on my shoulder, launches into a totally incomprehensible staccato rap. It's not just the accent, but every other word is, at least I imagine, medical jargon, because the students, nodding and scribbling, appear to understand what he's saying.

"Prognosis?" asks Louise.

"Louise," my doctor intervenes, "I think we can leave it there for the time being. Thank you all very much. Dr. Ho, if you wouldn't mind staying on, please."

The students, hugging their clipboards, are shown out by the nurse.

"Now, Mr. Green. Thank you very much for helping out. Much appreciated."

He looks down at the open folder on his desk.

"I see here, that the physio is extremely pleased with your progress."

"What progress would that be, Doctor? There's nothing going on down there. I mean nothing in the walking department."

"Oh, no," laughs Dr. Ho. "No walking department."

I look to my doctor, who shoots an exasperated glance in Ho's direction.

"We must not give up hope, Mr. Green, of course not.

However, in most instances of Guillain-Barré, including the variant you've contracted, we would expect if function was going to return, it would have done so within three to four months after the recovery had begun. And you're what, six months in?"

"So this is it?"

"I'm really very sorry, but I'm sure you wouldn't want me to offer false hopes, would you? Nothing is impossible, of course, and we will continue to do all we can for you, but…".

I close my eyes and stop listening. I want to scream. I want to cry. But more than anything, I want to get out of this room and away from my doctor's helplessness and Dr Ho's stupid, self-congratulatory smile.

Santa Is Waiting

Saturday, and after what seems a lifetime of low dripping clouds, the sky is clear blue. But trapped static in a wheelchair, I can't stay warm, the damn Russian wind slashes ice at my face and at my hands and at my legs. I've taken the kids down to the city on the bus. Together they pushed me from Castle Meadow to their demanded reward, MacDonald's. On the bus and all the way there we were attacked by a barrage of 'how cute' 'how adorable', 'aren't you lucky to have such lovely helpers' comments. By the time we got to the yellow arches I was ready to shoot the next person who even smiled a doggy-warm smile at us. It's tough enough being in a wheelchair without all that patronising crap being ladled on my head. Every day I am finding out more about the wonderful life of being a handicap… disabled person. If the quacks are right, there are going to be many more such days, bringing many more unwelcome lessons.

"How are we today?"

Oh hot jumping kreplach! This I don't need.

"We're fine and dandy, Mr. Motes."

"And who are these little angels?"

"This is Harley and Anna. And we, that's me and the little angels, need to be getting on now."

"You'd like your daddy to walk again, wouldn't you children?"

"He's not my daddy," says Harley.

"Listen, man, I am not in the market right now. In fact, I'll never be in the market. You see, I'm a Jew. We don't do Jesus. We don't do saints either."

"Why that's absolutely perfect! Perfect, praise the Lord! You see it was your people who crucified Him and also brought us St. William. To show His forgiveness, I am convinced if you come to Him he will cure you. Body and everlasting soul."

"Daddy, I want you to walk, like the man says. Can't you do please, Daddy?"

"You two stay here for a minute. I have to have a private word with Mr. Motes."

I grab him by the sleeve of his dark, threadbare suit and pushing my chair with one very pumped arm, and one very sore hand, I pull him into an off-balanced stumble away from the children.

"That crosses the line, you useless piece of crap. Shucking me is one thing, messing with my daughter is …".

"I am only the messenger. Only the messenger."

"Well, give the message to someone else, pal, because the next time you hit on me, and don't let this wheelchair fool you, you sorry putz, the next time I'll take your God-damed, holy-William message and shove it so far up your skinny ass that you'll have to squat and spread your cheeks to yodel."

Hello, Bobby Fishbaum! Where you been hiding out, man?

"God forgive you," he says as he backs away, all the

while keeping wary eyes fixed on me.

"Daddy, why did the man leave?"

"Urgent meeting I think."

"He said about walking. Will he do that."

"No, Pumpkin. The man is a little bit sick in the head. You know what I mean?"

She looks at me, hurt and disappointment flickering across her face.

"It's going to be fine, Anna. Come on now you two."

After wiping the remains of Big Macs, ketchup and fries from two small faces, it's my turn for a reward.

We're at a corner table in the relative warmth of Starbucks on Gentleman's Walk. The kids are having hot chocolate. Both are wearing frothy cream mustachios. I'm warming my hands around a very hot cup of fresh roasted black coffee. Heaven.

"Daddy, can we go to the toy store after?"

"We can go have a look, Pumpkin, but you'll have to wait for Christmas for Santa to come. It's only three weeks now."

"Oh, Daddy, three whole weeks! That's really, really a long time."

"We're going, my mum and dad and me, we're going to my Grandma Gwen for Christmas," pipes up Harley. "We're going to have a giant, giant tree," he says stretching his arms up, "and log fires and turkey too and lots of presents and …".

Behind the whipped cream, Anna's face begins to crumple.

"I don't care about animals," she says, her voice shaking. "I don't care if the President says to do. I don't, I don't. I want Mommy. I want her now. Right now. Please, Daddy. Please!"

Two bundled-up, middle-aged women at the next table stare and don't turn away when they see I've noticed. For sure not Brits.

I reach over to give Anna a hug. She crosses her arms and pulls away.

"What kind of animals are they," Harley asks, trying to puncture the tension.

Anna doesn't reply. She's flipped from miserable to angry.

I was really enjoying the coffee. Damn it!

"Anna, sweetheart, please stop now. Come on. Let Daddy finish his coffee and then we can all go across to the toy store. I'll give you each a pound to buy something. OK? Anna?"

She looks at me through her tears with no pity. Finally she relents with a curt nod.

"Pobrecita. Sin madre. Que lastima," one of the women says to her friend.

"Tambien con un un hombre discapacitado," the other adds, giving herself the luxury of a 'tisk tisk' for emphasis.

"Callate pinche bruja cabronas, lárgate de aquí," I mutter at them in my best LA Spanish.

Their mouths flap open. I start to say something else, but they're already in full retreat, out of their seats and out the door.

"What did you tell to those women," Harley asks, looking half way between scared and delighted.

"He called them ugly witches," Anna says gleefully. "Told them to shut up, which is very rude, Daddy. Didn't understand all of it."

That's a relief. At least she hasn't learned Chicano Spanish.

She starts to giggle, her pain momentarily forgotten.

"Wow! Wait until I tell Mum and Dad. Wow!"

"Come on, you two. Let's go to the toy store and see what we can see. Or we could go down to Jarrolds and visit Santa Claus. Wadda you say?"

"Father Christmas, Daddy. He's called Father Christmas."

"Right. Shall we visit Father Christmas then? Coats. Hats."

"Hello there, Bob."

I look up. A tall, attractive woman is standing by our table. I don't recognise her. What I do recognise is her three-quarter length Burberry wool coat and Isobel Marant boots. They were both very profitable knockoffs we brought in back home. She has her arm around a smooth-looking dude with slick-backed hair, graying at the temples. He's wearing a camelhair coat. That I don't recognise. From the way its cut, probably a Saville Row item.

"It's Delia, you know, Delia Castle."

Jesus, what a transformation.

"Of course it is. How you doing?"

"Just fine. This is my friend Maurice. Maurice this is Bob."

"Yes, hello, good to meet you " he says, looking right past me. "I'll get the coffees, darling."

He turns away and walks over to the counter. Nice guy. Real friendly.

"Sorry about that, Bob. Maurice is a bit on edge at the moment. Some business thing, I think."

"Whatever. No big deal. Nice to see you again, Delia. Listen, if I don't get these kids over to see Santa I'm going to have a small rebellion on my hands."

"Of course. Well, have a good time, children. Bye for now, Bob."

"So long," I call over my shoulder as the children propel me away at speed.

They don't want to keep Santa waiting and neither do I.

Blindsided

"Mr. Green, I know I told you on the phone this would be a good time, but an assignment has just come through, and I have to go off to London on the train and then on to Brussels first thing in the morning. You're going to have to excuse me if we make this very brief."

A very slight accent flavors her otherwise very precise English.

"Assignment?"

"Yes, I'm a freelance journalist. My agency wants me to file on the Common Agricultural Policy debate. Not the most interesting story, but…".

"Sure. Say, can you take your dog with you?"

"Of course I can. Norman's got his own passport."

Everything else has been so screwy, why not a dog with a passport. Maybe Norman takes notes for her.

"Is it difficult doing what you do?"

"Not at all," she says impatiently. "But I don't really have time right now for explaining the ins and outs of being a blind journalist, Mr. Green. So, if you could tell me what you want to know, we can get on and then I can get on."

Not a very friendly gal. Short and slight. Sensible clothes, sensible hairdo, sensible dark glasses. Maybe fashion isn't of much concern for blind people.

The apartment's living room is as sensibly boring as its owner. Two grey leather couches, two grey leather easy chairs, all sitting at right angles to each other on a nondescript brown carpet. The only thing on the walls is a large flat screen TV. No books, no tchatchkes, no pictures. Zip.

"Ben Castle's sister has asked me to talk to his friends to see if …".

"Yes, yes," she interrupts. "So you said when we spoke. I didn't know him very well and what I did know about him I didn't care for. A loudmouth, obnoxious drunk. I don't know how Janice put up with him, but then she was a very accepting person."

Unlike Sylvia Banning, who isn't. She's also sure as hell isn't worried about badmouthing the recently departed.

"Sure, I am with you on that one. One hundred percent. I'm trying to find out if there is some link between all the recent deaths. It might give me a clue whether Castle's death was accidental or not. If it's not too much to ask, could you fill me in a bit more on what happened to your friend?"

"Janice was my partner, Mr. Green, my civil partner."

"Got to excuse me, all this is new to me."

"Apparently so."

What is it with these people?

"Well, is there anything more you can tell me about what happened to your partner?"

"More than…?"

"More than Hedgy has. Said it was a freak accident. Said she was unlucky to be where she was when a hole opened up under the sidewalk."

Turning her back on me, she appears to be staring out

the window. We're eight storeys up, and there's great view over the city. I'm sure her partner, Accepting Janice, would have enjoyed it.

Norman, an enormous yellow Labrador, gets up from his cushion near one of the couches and goes over to stand beside his owner. He whines. She reaches down and strokes his head

"Not much more to tell. She went down that way every day, more of less the same time, to visit Pat, an old lady she was fond of. I know for a fact, a couple of times she had words with the builders about them blocking the pavement. Also complained to the Council. No one paid attention and then … Well, and then it happened."

"The accident?"

"The court will decide that. I say it was negligence, not an accident as such."

"You're suing then?"

"That's right. Suing the builders, the architect and the Council."

"I see. Well, I wish you luck."

She turns back to face me. Two thin lines of tears have escaped from behind the dark lenses. Norman looks up at her, his tail wagging.

"Anything else, Mr. Green? I really must get on now. Lots to do before I go."

"No, that's helpful. Thanks and, listen, have a good trip then."

She looks vaguely in my direction but says nothing.

Lost and Found

A distracted moment and Anna has disappeared. She was here, here right next to me not more than five seconds ago. I spin my chair but can't see her in the crush of people wandering about the art exhibition in the Forum. You don't get a great view sitting in a wheelchair, especially in crowds. Not now. Not now! I push my chair hard towards the door through a slowly shifting forest of legs, hoping to find her before she goes or is taken outside.

"Look out!" I shout at a ponderously-fat, middle-aged couple blocking my way.

"Terribly sorry," the man says, looking down. "Just because you're in a wheelchair doesn't give you the right to order people about, you know."

"Fuck you!" I shout, fear and frustration swamping my vow. Dad wouldn't mind. He adored his granddaughter.

"Really!" exclaims Mrs. Lardass. "Some people think the world owes them a living!"

Swinging sideways to get around them, I find myself confronted by two women yakking at each other while pushing baby strollers. They are more cooperative, break off talking and hurriedly move out of my way.

Still no Anna. I want to shout out Anna's name. Pointless. I see a policewoman standing at the side of the automatic door leading out of the building.

"Please, officer, have you seen a little girl?"

"I'm a WPC actually, sir."

"Fine, sorry, but my daughter has disappeared and …".

"There are rather a lot of children here, sir. What was she wearing?"

"Wearing? Yes. A green jacket, I think. And a wool hat. Green wool hat."

"Sorry, sir, I can't recall seeing a child matching that description. How old would she be?"

"Five. She's 5 years old."

"When did you last see her?"

"A few minutes ago. She was standing next to me, right next to me and then, then…".

"Then I wouldn't be too concerned, sir. I'm sure she's around here somewhere. Children do wander. If you like, I would be willing to accompany you to look for her. What's your daughter's name?"

"Anna. Her name's Anna."

We start to move through the crowd. Nothing. It must be at least five minutes now. I see a flash of green and push towards it. No. Not her. Anna! Oh Christ!

"Let me contact a colleague."

She mutters something into the microphone attached to her uniform near her mouth. Static spits back.

As we pass an open staircase I almost bump in to someone in an electric wheelchair. It's Brendan. He throws a spastic hand up at me. A greeting? Do I care? I don't. I start to push past. Again the hand. I stop.

"Daddy!"

She's standing next to him, her hand on his arm.

I reach out for her. She runs into my arms. I try not to, but can't stop the sobs of relief. I hug her.

"Daddy, you alright? Daddy? Don't cry, Daddy."

"As I said, sir, she hadn't gone far. You need to stay with your father, Anna. He was very very worried about you."

Anna stares open-mouthed at the policewoman. She touches her hat, turns and moves away.

"I couldn't find you, Daddy. I looked and looked and then I saw this man, Brendan is his name. I saw Brendan and thought he would know you because he has a wheelchair, and it's much, much better than your wheelchair. It's an electrical chair. But, Brendan, he said he didn't know you. He said I could wait with him and that you would find us. He's very nice, Brendan is."

"He sure is, Sweetheart."

How the hell could she understand what he'd said to her?

"Thanks very much, Brendan, I really appreciate what you did."

He says something I can't fathom.

"That's great, Brendan," I reply, hoping that's the answer he's looking for.

He turns and garbles at Anna.

"Brendan says if you don't know what he says, just ask him to say again."

"Sorry, Brendan. I guess it happens to you all the time. It must be a total pain in the ass."

His blue eyes sparkle. His body twists as he grins

broadly and slams himself backwards in the chair. Then he garbles again. Anna looks little-kid serious before being attacked by a storm of giggles.

"Brendan says you look like you've been hit by a bus, Daddy."

"How did you know?"

More slam-dunk hilarity.

"Come on," I say. "Do you have time to let me buy you a cup of coffee?"

"Thank you," he replies.

It's the first words from him I have understood. Might be hope for me after all.

Coffee with Brendan

Brendan has extracted a thick plastic straw from the side of his wheelchair seat. He flaps about until it's in his mouth and then bends forward in a well-practiced jerky motion before the end of the straw finds the coffee cup. He slurps up the coffee in two or three long sucks. Quite a performance.

We are sitting in the cafe inside the Forum's atrium. At the far end of the open exhibition space is a separate entrance to the library. All is contained in a three-story, glass-fronted building that looks out on a large medieval church. Best of all, the coffee is excellent, even better than Starbucks.

Anna is concentrating on a tall glass of Coke. I'm concentrating on trying to catch what Brendan is saying.

"Afraid," he spits out.

For my benefit he is saying one word at a time, as if he was talking to a slow-witted, non-English speaker. That would be me.

"Can't - understand? Don't - be - afraid. Can't - understand - if - afraid."

How could I be afraid of this guy? No way. He can't even button his own shirt. Well, yeah. Maybe he's right. After all, he is my nightmare cripple, all random twitches, mangled speech and out-of-context drooling. Much worse than strapped-up Ronald. At least I could understand him.

"Where's your helper?" I ask.

"Assistant. Personal - assistant."

After our first meeting, I know how touchy he can be. I play the game.

"Your personal assistant then. Where is he?"

"Henry?"

"Yeah, the black guy."

"Off."

"Off?"

"Don't - need - him - all - day."

This is better. I relax. He does too and begins rattling away. I'm right back to square one. I raise my arms in surrender. Luckily my translator is well tuned in.

"Brendan says you look more comfortable in the wheelchair," Anna says.

"Oh, right. Thanks. I hope it's going to be just a temporary thing."

His entire body contorts with laughter.

"I've - been - disabled - all - my - life. Harder - for - you - new - boys."

Yeah. Strangely, besides all the usual shit you need to figure out when you're a new kid in a wheelchair - how to open a door, how to transfer over to a toilet, how to negotiate going up and down curb cuts without tipping over - the one thing I find most disturbing is the view. I was six-three. Guess I still am. The world very different. Now instead of faces or tops of heads, I am forced to gaze on a bewildering parade of asses, legs and crotches. I have a permanent stiff neck from having to look up to talk to people. At least with Brendan, even with all the garble, we're on the same level, face to face.

"You bet it is, Brendan."

"Harley!" Anna shouts. "Over here. Over here."

Harley and his parents have just come into the Forum. They all stop when they hear Anna.

The little boy runs over to us. Molly and Paddy trail behind.

"Brendan," says Anna, "this is my very bestest friend, Harley. Harley, this is my new friend, Brendan."

Harley gives Brendan a frightened glance, then looks over at his parents for reassurance.

"OK," Brendan says, "I've - had - lunch."

Like the first time I met him, a regular comedian.

Paddy and Molly come over, all tats, leather, wild hair and piercings, and stand next to us. Now it's Brendan's turn to look worried.

"I reckon they've had their lunch too," I say to him.

Once again, Brendan doubles up and slams back alarmingly. Not only a comedian, but one with a sense of the ridiculous, even at his own expense.

I introduce Paddy and Molly. Paddy seems uncertain. Molly straight away sticks out her hand and waits patiently for Brendan to catch it. After a couple of wild swings they connect.

"Nice meeting you, Anna's new friend."

Brendan grin is so bright it transforms him into a human lightbulb.

Paddy seems wrong footed and embarrassed.

"You want to come with us to the Children's Library, Anna?" Molly asks.

Harley puts out a hand. Anna takes it.

"Bring her back directly, Greenie," Paddy says. "You'll be wanting a ride home, will you?"

"Yes, thanks, Paddy. That would be great."

It's just me and Brendan. No translator.

Word by word, he asks me where I from in California, why I'm living in Norwich, where Anna's mother is, what I do for a living. I give him what I hope is a plausible tale.

Although it's hard to tell with all the head shakes and facial moves, Brendan's sharp look say he's not all that convinced. Thankfully, he doesn't push it. Then he tells me his tale.

He was born south of London and sent away to a special boarding school for children like himself when he was six years old. Hell, Anna is only a year younger. I would just as soon send her away from home as cut off my arm. Poor bastard! When he finally got out of there at eighteen he was dumped in a home with a load of other handicapped people somewhere out in the boonies.

"Couldn't - go - anywhere. Boring - boring - boring. One - person - to - feed - three - disabled - people. Food - really - awful!"

Finally, when he was in his mid-twenties someone came to the home and taught him to use a computer. Over the web he was able to enlist the help of an advocate. She arranged to get him out and fixed up an apartment for him in Norwich with his own personal assistants. Now he made his living by designing websites, teaching and working out adaptations so other handicapped people could use computers. Looking at him, I can't imagine how he operates a computer, but what the hell do I know.

"Independence -real - life - respect," he says with a big smile.

"I hear you, Brendan. Respect is where it should be at for everybody."

"So - not - handicapped - but - disabled - people. Respect. Like African - American. Respect. Disabled - people. Yes?"

I give up.

"You got it, Brendan.

Snake Eyes

The Chinese guy pats me on the shoulder. "Tough luck, New Blood," he says.

"Yeah. Well, it goes like that sometimes. But, thanks for letting me sit in fellas. Appreciate it."

"If you want to play again, son, you're always welcome," the florid-faced antique dealer adds, grinning like a wolf.

The other four guys around the baize-covered table, a used car dealer leaking big flakes of dandruff onto his collar, a bearded musician, a heavy-betting accountant and a guy who looks like Minnesota Fats, all nod in agreement.

And why the hell not? This New Blood, this LA cardsharp, this total schmuck has just had his clock cleaned for £200. Ordinarily I could live with that, although ordinarily I wouldn't have to, but out of a £500 bankroll, this one really hurts.

My first mistake was figuring I could leverage May Quest's money into something more interesting by hooking myself up with a card game. My next mistake was asking Paddy if he knew where I could find some action.

"Don't know if they're still at it, but my dad used to play almost every week with a bunch of old boys at the back of a Chinese chippy on Dereham Road. Lots of money on the table. You up for that kinda thing, Greenie?"

What the hell would a bunch of old Norwich guys know about real poker? After all, I'd regularly got up from the table in LA with at least a few thousand more than I sat down with. I also did pretty good in Vegas playing against strangers.

Now, I'm not saying I was a hot shot poker player. I knew my limitations and always made sure I played within them. I learned all the moves from my uncle, 'Atlantic City' Sol.

"It ain't a pissing contest," he had told me when I started out. "Let the schmucks show what kinda big men they are, make the big fancy bets, puff out their chests, flash their wads. You, Bobby, you watch, you wait, you play the odds, nibble a little maybe here and a little there. No big showboat crap. Nobody will notice that you went home with more than you came with. The secret is to let people underestimate you. If they do, then you got 'em by the balls and they'll never feel you squeezing."

From when I rolled up to the table and saw the first hand dealt I knew I had underestimated these old farts, big time. I also knew beyond a doubt that my balls were going to be squeezed and, more, I knew I was going to feel it.

"Sure sorry about that, Greenie," Paddy says, as we drive home. "I told you they'd been playing together for a long time."

"Wasn't my game, Paddy. Texas Hold'em is what we play back home. Seen, but never played seven-card stud before tonight."

"It's still poker, no?"

"Yeah, same value hands, but the way it's dealt and the way the hands play out and the betting are all totally different. Like the difference between billiards and pool."

"Yeah, I saw that one. Paul Newman wasn't it?"

"That's right, but Fast Eddie worked it out and beat that rich guy in the end."

"So, you're no Fast Eddie and this ain't no film."

"Only got myself to blame for screwing up so bad. I ignored every rule I'd learned about playing cards. Especially the one big one."

"Which is?"

"Never gamble to put food on the table."

"It ain't that bad, is it?"

"Not yet, but if something doesn't turn up soon, it will be. I told you Tina took off with my stash, more than ten grand."

"Pounds?"

"No, dollars, but what difference does it make now."

"Bloody hell, Greenie. I knew she ripped you off, but not so bad."

"It is what it is, Paddy. I know it doesn't look like it right now, what with what's been going on, but something good will turn up. Has to. You can't keep rolling snake eyes forever, can you?"

Out of Jail Free

"Mr. Green. Oh, Mr. Green."

I am caught while pushing myself up the ramp to the side entrance of City Hall. With the remainder of Legless Ben's sister's money, that I'd wisely put aside before getting my ass kicked in that god-damned poker game, I can now pay off at least some of the back rent I've run up and then, hopefully, the threatening letters, even though they're still addressed to the missing Tina Malloy, will stop dropping through the mail slot. If I could get Richards off my back as well, I would sleep a whole lot better. Apparently, that's going to be more tricky.

"Detective Sergeant, I thought you had finished with me. More routine questions about Ben Castle? Or that bus thing?"

"No, Mr. Green, I think we've managed to just about conclude our investigations on those incidents. I'm afraid we've got another one, however. When you finish in there would you mind popping by the station for a few minutes?"

What to do but pop, as requested. So, after I part with £150 at the rent cashier's window, I roll up the road to the police station and ask to see Sergeant Richards.

Richards looks different. His combover is neatly combed over, his suit coat unrumpled and his pants sharply pressed. He seems way too pleased with himself, jaunty even. I tell myself it has nothing to do with me, that maybe he's found romance. However, my father told me never to trust a cop, any cop, but especially a cop who looked as if he just won second prize in a beauty contest. Dad and Uncle Sol were both crazy for Monopoly. That and pinochle.

"Thanks very much for coming, Mr. Green. Sorry to bother you once again, but something has come up that I think you may be able to help us with."

He leads the way to an interview room at the back of the police station. No windows, pastel blue walls, a table and three metal folding chairs. The only concession to bleakness is indirect lighting. I figure he'll wheel in the hot lights when I refuse to confess.

"Cup of tea?"

"No, thanks, I'm good."

"About an hour or so ago I returned from Accident and Emergency where a Mr. Saunders, a wheelchair-bound disabled person, is being treated for multiple stab wounds."

"Am I now in the frame for anything that happens to every handicapped person in the damn city? Come on, Detective Sergeant, get real, will yah."

"Oh, I am real, Mr. Green, real interested why your name has come up yet again."

"You gotta be kidding me, man, I mean Sergeant. I don't even know anyone, handicapped or normal, named Saunders."

"That is curious, because he seems to know you. Said he met you the other day at the Centre. Didn't know your name, but described you as 'A big Yank in a wheelchair' is what he said.' Of course, there may be some other big Yank in a wheelchair, but one of the staff did say that Mr. Saunders had recently had a visit from someone calling himself Bob Green."

"Brendan?"

"No, Christian name is Martin. When I asked him if he had noticed anything or anyone unusual recently, standard procedure in cases like this, particularly as the attack occurred right outside the Centre, you were the only new person he remembers seeing in the last few weeks."

"Oh, him. Yeah, I did talk with a guy named Martin, a little handicapped fella in a wheelchair. Only spoke to him for a few minutes though. Haven't seen him since."

"Can I ask what you wanted to speak to Mr. Saunders about?"

"I didn't want to talk to him at all. I only met him as I was leaving."

"And?"

"And we were just passing the time of day. Someone told me I should go up there and see what kinda stuff they had going for people like me. So we were chewing the fat, one wheelchair guy to another."

Richards gives me an unsettling cop stare.

"Did he know who knifed him?" I ask.

"I'm afraid not. Happened after dark. Lucky for him the cleaners came out when they did, else he may not have survived. As it is, he'll be in the hospital for a few more days. He's cut up pretty bad."

"Sorry to hear that. He seemed a decent guy. Any idea why he was attacked?"

"The investigation is ongoing, but looks like it may have been a mugging gone wrong. They got away with his wallet and his mobile and a couple of rings as well. He was very upset about the rings."

Richards places his hands on the table and leans over so his face is on the same level as mine.

"Does it not strike you as curious, Mr. Green, that you have met recently with two disabled people, one who we find soon after in the river and the next one who is viciously attacked, and but for his leather jacket and his attacker being disturbed would now also be dead?"

Curious for sure. I toy with reminding him of Legless Ben's list, but as they haven't wheeled out the hot lights, I figure for now pleading ignorance is a better bet.

"You implying I had something to do with this, Detective or with what happened to Ben Castle? Come on now, really."

"Of course not. However, as I'm sure you'll understand, we have to be thorough and follow any leads that we have."

I look at him and smile, hold out both hands, palms up and give him a Yiddishe shrug. Richard seems perplexed. Probably never seen one of these before in Norwich.

"Thanks very much for your help. Mr. Green. That'll be all for now."

Never underestimate the power of Out of Jail Free shrug. My dad and my uncle would be proud.

More Coffee with Brendan

"Hey Brendan, how's it hanging?"

"It's hanging by a bloody thread."

"My turn to get the coffee."

"You sure?"

"Sure."

It's exactly a week since we last met up at the Forum cafe. That was our second meeting. I'd come here to keep an eye on Anna and Harley while Molly went shopping. The kids stampeded into the Children's Library. Since they couldn't leave the building without passing the cafe, I went out there for a cup of coffee. On the way I bumped into Brendan - literally. He'd come zipping around the corner of the DVD racks and smacked into the side of my chair. He twisted and flailed with laughter, then apologized, then invited me for coffee. After that we agreed to meet the following week. Despite all the off-the-wall, drooling-crazy cripple shit, Brendan was sort of growing on me. He was surprisingly sharp and funny. What my dad would have called, 'a regular mensch'.

"Where's Anna at?"

"She and her friend, Harley, they're in the library, like last week, getting new books."

"Nice little girl. You're lucky," he says wistfully. "Little ones are usually the best."

"How's that?"

"So much is brand new for them. Until they learn

different, they take the world as they find it."

"Meaning you, Brendan?"

"Not only me."

"One thing I have noticed, is that kids will often come and ask me why my legs don't work or why I use a wheelchair, but before I can answer their parents rush over and pull them away."

"That's it. Embarrassed. Or maybe we scare them."

What's this 'we' bullshit? Strapped-up Ronald also wanted to include me in his club. However, as someone said, I don't want to be a member of a club that wants me for a member, especially the Norwich Cripples' Club.

"Brendan, got a question for you. Do you know a disabled guy called Ronald? Ran into him at rehab physiotherapy."

"Is there some reason you think disabled people in Norwich should all know each other?"

"Not really. Just wondered, that's all."

"Matter of fact, Bob, I do know him. Bomber Burns. A right nutter he is."

"How so?"

"Ex-Army, you know, thinks we should obey the rules and all that. Never approved of what we were doing. Called us gormless agitators. Got no time for him."

"I didn't think he was so bad. Kinda liked him in fact. Sparky he was. A funny guy."

"If you mean funny peculiar, you got that right."

"No, like amusing funny. Thought you two would hit it off."

"Yeah, well, we don't. But still and all, the town's big enough for both of us. We don't meet up very often, which is more than fine with me."

"Right. I see. One more for you then. Have you ever been bugged by this guy called Motes. Priest or ex-priest. Wanted to…".

"Make you walk," slam laughs Brendan. "Asks all of us that."

There he goes again with the 'us' shit.

"And?"

"We tell him, it's people like him and his Christian charity rubbish that makes life tough for us, not our wheelchairs or our impairments. Caught two or three of us on the Market one time and we ran him off with our chairs. Called out for God to forgive us, but he kept going."

"Nice one."

Brendan is all smiles, of which he owns a big-time solid one.

"Say, you hang out here a lot?" I ask.

"Wednesday afternoons. Time off from the Centre. Too much time with computers makes Brendan a dull boy."

"You work there? I figured you were, you know."

"A social service client?"

"Ah, yeah, more or less. Yeah."

"'Course you did. Disabled garble, garble…".

"Sorry, Brendan, I didn't get that part, right after 'disabled'.

"People, disabled people don't have jobs. Right?"

"No, that's not it," although it was. "I figured with what that Mr. Yallop said, something about a duty of care, that he was looking after you."

"Sometimes he thinks he does."

"From what I've heard, he's not doing all that well with the 'looking after' bit."

Brendan gives me an appraising look.

"I heard that Martin Saunders had been attacked a couple of days ago. Is he going to be OK?"

Brendan looks uneasy, suddenly more twitchy, if that were possible for a guy who seems to be in perpetually twitchy motion.

"Who said?"

"Cops did. Because I had a few words with him as I left the Centre, you know that time I came to see you, they thought I could give them some information, which I couldn't."

"He'll live. Tough guy is Martin. Bit of a pillock, if you know what I mean. Underneath all that, he's a diamond, rough diamond."

"Brendan, listen. I didn't want to bring it up before, 'cause I know you were really upset, but now with what's happened to Martin, can we talk about what's been going on with all the accidents?"

"That's the thread I was on about. You know I'm the only one of the Rollers who hasn't been touched. Yet."

"Well, yeah. You talking about Ben Castle's list?"

Brendan swivels his head around and then jerks himself forward so that his face is close to mine.

"Not here. Not safe here. I've been working on something though. Should have it done tomorrow. Can you come over to the Centre on Friday, late morning? We can talk then."

Jail is Not Very Wheelchair Friendly

"Mr. Green? I thought I made clear to you that we can't have people coming into the Centre and disturbing our members. We have a duty to protect …".

"Hold your horses, Mr. Yallop. It is Yallop? Good. Brendan asked me to come visit him here. I assume that's alright? He wanted to show me his computer room."

"I see. Well technically, it's not 'his computer room' as such. No, the computer room belongs to the Centre. Brendan's only in charge of instructing, that's all. But, if he asked you to come, I suppose that will have to do for now."

"Well, thank you very much, Mr. Yallop. How very considerate of you."

"Please, but there is no call for taking such a sarcastic tone, Mr. Green."

"I know, you're only doing your job. Right?"

He looks down at me. I look up at him and can almost hear an angry whinny accompanying the grotesque flaring of his nostrils. If you ignore the too-generous nose hair, I am looking into two tunnels or maybe the business end of a double-barrelled shotgun.

"I would appreciate it, however," he says huffily, "if you were to limit yourself to discussing computers, especially after what recently happened to poor Martin Saunders after you spoke to him. I assume you've heard about the incident?"

"Oh yeah. Indeed I did. I even had a talk with the police, for which I suppose I have you to thank."

"Well, I was only …".

"Doing you job?"

With a parting snort from out of the bushy tunnels, Yallop does a military about face and strides off, his footfalls echoing loudly as he marches down the linoleumed corridor.

Three old women in wheelchairs, I'm sure the same three Furies who were there on my last visit, follow his progress until he disappears into a side room. Then, as if their heads were attached to a single neck, the three faces swivel around to stare at me. I smile at them. They don't smile back. Furies don't do smiles. Their gig is vengeance.

Having rolled past the unwelcoming dragon and smiled down the Furies, I roll into Brendan's sizeable computer room, adjacent to the Centre's front door. A dozen computers are set up on two parallel facing tables under harsh florescent lighting. One tube is flickering on and off. Brendan is working at one of the machines. He's wearing a headset with a round black sensor protruding in front of his face from a flexible stalk attached to a band around his head. Henry is sitting next to him.

A computer voice greets me with "Hi, Bob Green. Are you well today?"

The same message flashes up on an LED news ticker on the wall behind Brendan.

"Fine and dandy, Hal. Just don't toss me out of the airlock."

"Don't like it much either," Brendan says with a chuckle

and his own voice. "Good enough for Stephen Hawking, but he's got no choice."

Since our third chat in the Forum cafe, my fear level dropped away and, as he had predicted, my understanding of his garble grew until I had become almost bilingual in English and Brendan. Naturally, I couldn't speak Brendan.

"Nice setup, Brendan. Where are all your students today?"

"Mystery tour in the dribble bus."

"In the what bus?"

"Dribble bus. You know, fill it up with disabled people and off they go, dribbling all the way there and all the way back."

There is a real twisted sense of humor in that twisted body.

"You said you wanted to see me, Brendan. What can I do for you?"

He says something to Henry, who walks past me and shuts the door. Brendan motions me to come closer.

"It's more about what I can do for you and maybe me as well," he whispers. "I want to talk about the list, Ben's list. I'm the only one left. Like I told you the other day, I figure I must be next."

"Everyone says there is no list. His wife said so, the police, even your buddy Martin told me there wasn't any list."

Henry hands me a yellow ring binder. Inside are a bunch of pages of what look like official documents. The heading on the first page reads:

Norfolk Constabulary Crime Report

I flip through the documents. All concern the deaths of Brendan's wheelchair gang. All, except for the last two, have Closed in big red letters stamped across them. The first of these exceptions is a report on my run-in with the bus. Case Ongoing it says. The report of the attack on Martin is also marked as ongoing. The final two pages are a long additional note written by DS Richards. In it he proposes reopening all the cases. 'Despite initial conclusions that these disabled people were accident victims, as more incidents have occurred I am requesting that all cases be immediately reopened and we make efforts to see if, besides the fact that all victims were wheelchair bound, there is a common thread that connects these cases or a common perpetrator who may be responsible for these incidents. Further, I feel a full review of all the items found at the incident scenes may reveal important information.' At the bottom of the second page someone has scrawled in green ink, 'Request denied,' and under that in smaller print 'need to prioritise scarce resources'.

"How in God's name did you get this stuff?"

Brendan raises a shaky finger towards his lips.

I repeat the question, this time more quietly.

Brendan looks at his computer screen.

"Just like that? Anyone can find this stuff by using a computer?"

"You don't know much about computers, do you?"

"That's an understatement, my friend. I mean, you know, I've used email and the internet but that's about it."

Henry whisper's something and Brendan shakes his head.

"No," he says. "Tell him."

Henry seems doubtful.

"You must never tell anyone about this, Bob Green," Henry says. "Not a soul. I didn't think he should tell you, but Brendan insists. I don't know why, but he says you can be trusted. The fact is that Brendan here is a first-rate hacker. One of the best there is or ever was or is ever likely gonna be. A legend if the truth be told. But best it's not told. Usually he just goes in and leaves his tag, or does favours for people who need a helping hand, but for something like this…".

"And he got this stuff from where?"

"The police computer system. That's right. As I was saying, for something like this he had to go in and leave no tags, no footprints, not a trace he was ever there. So, you must never mention or even hint at this to anyone. You understand how serious this is?"

"You bet I do."

"Jail's not very wheelchair friendly," Brendan adds.

"Neither is whoever's bumping off your buddies."

The Wrong Einstein

The Manpig's trench coat is belted and buttoned. Thank God! At least I won't have to deal with Hedgy's Internal Rabbis.

The man himself clumps unsteadily across the studio to meet me.

"Hello, Bob. How are we today? "

He's wearing a three-quarter length blue velvet dress and four-inch platform shoes, perfect for unsteady clumping. Besides the pearl-drop earrings, the only other jewellery is a single string of pearls. Very elegant. Lots of dark eyeshadow and soft ruby lipstick. Today's wig is a black pageboy and the hearing-aid flowers are small daisies. From where I'm sitting it's impossible to see if there's a yarmulke hanging on up there.

"You going to introduce your friend?"

"Sure thing. Sorry. This is Paddy, my next-door neighbor."

"Driver and minder as well," says Paddy.

"Delighted," Hedgy says, putting out a hand.

Poor Paddy seems not to know whether to shake it or kiss it. He does neither.

Brendan and Henry, together with Martin are on the far side of the studio next to the river-view window. We go over to join them. Brendan has asked us to meet up, saying only that he wanted to talk about what's been happening. No mention of the documents or Richards' memo.

"Paddy, you met Brendan at the Forum. This is Martin and Henry, Brendan's assistant."

"Morris," says Henry. "It's Morris."

"Morris?"

"Henry's twin brother. We both work for Brendan. Shifts."

"Right, sorry."

"No worries, mate. Happens all the time."

Martin's face is bruised and pieces of black duct tape on his leather jacket show where he was knifed.

Introductions finally navigated, I ask him how he's feeling.

"Better. Sore though. Still got rows of stitches in me. Wankers!! Took my rings too. Bloody wankers! I could have sorted them out too, if they hadn't snuck up behind me. Didn't have a chance, creeping up on me like they done."

"Easy, big man," cautions Hedgy. "You'll bust those stitches if you're not careful."

"What do you know about it?" Martin squeaks at Hedgy. "You wasn't there, was you?"

"Cut it out you two," Brendan says, trying to throw his hands up and succeeding only in flailing them about. "This is too serious."

"If it's so serious," says Hedgy, "where's Sylvia, and where's the fragrant Mrs. Castle?"

As if on cue, the door opens and Sylvia and Norman come in.

"Apologies," she says. "Had to finish a last minute

article. Can someone tell me who else is here?"

Hedgy laces her arm through his, guides her across the room and makes the introductions.

"Delia?" Hedgy asks. "The only one missing."

"Morris did call her," Brendan says, "but she said she was too busy. Something like that anyway."

"Should I tell them what she actually said?" Morris asks.

"Why not," Brendan replies.

"She said she'd had enough of disabled people to last her two lifetimes. Then she slammed the phone down."

"I heard," adds Morris, "that she's had all Ben's adaptations chucked into a skip in front of the house. Hand rails, shower chair, even the stairlift's been ripped out."

"That's not very friendly," Hedgy pouts. "I'd thought better of her."

"Well," says Brendan, "Ben was not very nice to her."

"Em, suppose that's true enough," admits Hedgy.

"Not nice?" Sylvia spits, "Not nice? What he was, was a total bastard. Treated his wife like shit. Come on you lot, tell it like it is, or was."

No one contradicts her, although Hedgy raises his eyebrows and makes a sour face, which, of course, Sylvia can't see.

"Martin, any more from the police?" Brendan asks.

"You having a laugh, mate? They come up to hospital a couple of times to ask questions, but since I've been out, not a dickie bird. Reckon Norfolk coppers ain't much cop at all."

Martin giggles. No one else seems to find it funny. I don't get the joke.

"Will you for once pack it in with the phony Cockney!" Hedgy snaps. "You're from Swaffham, for God's sake, Martin, not the East End."

"Oh right. And I suppose you'd know all about the East End, would you? We talkin' Bow Bells and Bagels?"

"I would say that such a remark was beneath you, Mr. Saunders, but, as anyone can see, there's not much room to fit much of anything beneath you."

"You over-dressed deaf ponce!"

"Bloody Nora!" Brendan splutters. "Don't you two understand? Can't you see that something is going on? We've got no time for squabbling."

Silence. After a few moments, Brendan continues.

"Even Bob, who was asking questions about what's happening, has been targeted. Pushed right out in front of a bus for his efforts. Stands to reason that somebody's trying to wipe us out. Why else Bob? Why else one Rolling Dervish after another? What's more, I've heard that at least one copper is thinking along the same lines. Even wants to reopen all the cases to see if they're connected in some way."

"Don't know about that," Hedgy replies. "I mean, look what happened to my Sarah. Murdered by that bloody, infernal machine. It didn't attack Martin. It didn't dig that hole for Janis. It didn't wheel Ben into the river."

"Hedgy!" Brendan garble-shouts. "Not now."

"You never did believe me, did you?" he huffs. "None of you really believed me."

Martin and Brendan stare at him. Sylvia grimaces and shakes her head. He coughs nervously, reaches up to touch his wig, then pulls down the hem of his skirt.

"OK, OK! Yes, yes, yes. Who then?" he says, looking defeated.

"That's what we need to find out," Brendan says, "before we're all murdered in our chairs."

"Well, for what it's worth, my vote goes to old man Yallop," Martin says. "To be honest, the wanker never did take to us getting together and making all the bother 'bout wanting to run things for ourselves. Was always going on how we couldn't be doing this, how we couldn't be doing that, how he and his staff was responsible, and what would they say if anything happened and then when it did happen, how he'd been right all along."

"He is a nasty piece of work, I agree with you on that," Hedgy says, "but, at least from what I've seen of him, not a clever enough nasty piece of work to orchestrate everything that's happened. No, not Yallop. If I had to point a finger," he says, droopingly aiming a red-lacquered finger at Martin, "it would be at those simply darling people who ran that care home we helped you and Barry to escape from. After Sarah and I snuck in Brendan's little spy cams and you two told the inspectors about all the abuse, they were not only closed down, but three of them wound up in prison. Now there's the reason for a real grudge."

"One problem with that," Brendan replies, "is the last

time I heard they were still up at the prison."

"Maybe their family then," Hedgy ventures. "Didn't they have a couple of boys? Big lads they were. Saw them at the trial."

"Evil bastards that family, without a shadow, evil bastards," Martin counters. "But, despite what you're saying Hedge, the lot of 'em makes Yallop look like bleeding Alfred Einstein."

"I think you'll find that's Albert Einstein," Hedgy observes archly.

"Up yours, you total wanker!"

I am finding it difficult to see how the Rolling Dervishes had ever posed a threat to anyone, except maybe each other.

"I think you're all out of your minds," Sylvia says. "How could anyone have fixed the pavement so Janice went into that hole? Impossible."

"Maurice Piper," Brendan snaps.

"Now they're on about potatoes," Paddy mutter-laughs softly. "Talk about not being able to organise a pissup in a brewery."

Strangely, besides myself, it is only deaf Hedgy, who is looking directly at Paddy, that picks up what he says.

"Not potatoes, Motorcycle Man," he laughs. "That would be Maris Piper. Brendan is referring to Maurice Piper, the architect."

"Wanker." Martin adds helpfully.

"You might be on to something there with that, Brendan," Hedgy says.

"Anyone want to let us in on the secret?"

"A little over a year ago," Hedgy explains. "The Rollers complained about the lack of proper disabled access and convinced the planning people to knock back a big development of a sports complex Piper designed. It's costing his firm a fortune, maybe two hundred thousand or so to put it right. He was really fuming. Told the newspaper that the disabled knew nothing about proper architecture and should leave things to the experts."

"Yeah," Brendan laughs, crashing himself backwards in his chair, "remember how at the planning meeting he blew up and called us all pathetic, welfare-scrounging, nit-picking whingers."

"Wanker!"

"A few weeks later we lost Janis," Brendan says.

"What's more," Sylvia adds, "who do you think the architect is I'm suing over what happened to her? Yes. That's right. Maurice Piper."

"That's all interesting," I say, "but there's a long stretch between being pissed off and murdering folks. So, if all you've got are suspicions and speculation, then what you've got is bubkis."

They all stare at me.

"Oh, yeah. Pardon my Yiddish. Nothing is what you've got, at least as far as the cops are concerned. Any real hard, smoking-gun evidence on Piper or on Yallop or on those resident-home people?"

The three look at each other. Sylvia pats Norman's head. No one says a word.

Follow the Money

"**Y**our wheelchair mates, the blind bird and that deaf bloke in the dress are all bleeding hopeless," Paddy laughs.

We're driving home from Hedgy's studio. Unable to come up with more than a list of who might want to get rid of them, they soon descended once more into quarrelling, heavily laced with recriminations and put downs.

"No argument there, Paddy."

"Tell me, Don Corleone, how would you big-time gangsters be after dealing with this kinda thing?"

"Paddy, do I look like a big-time gangster to you? Or any kind of gangster? Come on, man. I told you already, my family were mostly on the sidelines of all that violence crap. Bit part players is what they were. The only one who you might have thought of as being really heavy was Great-Great-Grandpa Abe, the legendary first Fishbaum, who came to America from Odessa, and then you only had to worry about him if you were a horse."

"I remember that one. Yeah, the head in the bed thing."

"No, man, like if the stableman or iceman or delivery man or milkman didn't pay protection, his horse would drop down dead from something it ate. Most guys paid up. Horse poisoning was a pretty good racket back then."

"I love it!" he says banging his hands hard against the

steering wheel. "I bloody love it."

"Yeah, funny, Paddy, very funny."

"Sorry, Greenie. You gotta admit it ain't the kinda thing you'd find hanging off of most people's family tree."

"My family tree, and what is or isn't hanging from it, is not going to help unravel who is wasting wheelchair people in Norwich, is it?"

Wait up now. Thinking about the family, I remember Grandpa Nathan, who did something - my father always insisted it was a non-lethal something - with Bugsy Siegel in Vegas. Although I can't imagine how anything to do with Bugsy Seigel could have been non-lethal.

When I knew him, he was still a snappy casino dresser, but with rotten breath, a vein-mapped face and using a throat vibrator. I also figure, at least I do now, that he was short a few bones in his dominoes' pile.

Often, and out of any apparent context, he would grab my arm, pull me close, flooding my face with old-man's breath and in a throat-vibrated whisper tell me, "Bubbala, you wanna get ahead in this life? You wanna know what's what? Who's on first? Who's on second? Do you?"

I was maybe six or seven. I had not a clue what the scary old guy was talking about.

"Then you always follow the money. Always, the money. You hear me, my darling little boychick? On gelt iz keyn velt. Without money there is no world."

Thanks, Grandpa Nathan.

"The money, Paddy. Maybe that's where we need to start."

175

"What are you on about now, Greenie? What money?"

"Simple. Who has the most to gain, money wise, by murdering these people?"

"No bloody idea, mate."

"Well, neither do I, at least not for all of them. However, I do know for a fact that Hedgy got almost a million from the wheelchair company. Delia, that's Legless Ben's wife, she got a shitload of money and a house to boot. Sylvia Banning, the blind lady, she's suing the Council and the builders and that architect. Lots of money there."

"Don't know about the wife or the blind bird, Greenie, but going on all them paintings, that poof in the dress seemed pretty hung up on his old lady."

"That's true enough, but then love and hate are pretty damn close to each other. Maybe they had a falling out. Maybe she was going to go off with someone who doesn't wear women's clothes. Don't know about Sylvia. Hard to figure out how she could have done away with Janice the way it happened. As far as Ben Castle is concerned, if I were Delia, I would have pushed him into the river a long time ago."

"Interesting theory, Greenie, but think on it a bit more. Except for the legless bloke's old lady, how could the others be knowing there was money in killing them people? Don't seem likely, at least to me it don't."

"Yeah, didn't think about that, but then maybe after Janice died and Sylvia began to sue all those people, couldn't the others have started thinking they might be on to a good thing if they arranged accidents they

176

could blame on somebody or on a company with lots of money?"

"Don't know, Greenie. Seems a stretch to me. Like how does it fit that little bloke being carved up, or what you told me about the crazy wheelchair thing with that woman? Thin I'd call it, real thin."

"Yeah, I guess so. Like you say, too much of a stretch."

All that wise grandfather shit, delivered in a mist of halitosis, and what have I got from it? Just like the others, bubkis is what I've got. Thanks for nothing, Grandpa Nathan.

Chickens in the Rain

"I'll take both of them out to my mum's place in Suffield for the weekend," Molly says. "They'll have a great time and Mum, she loves little ones."

"Yeah she does an' all," adds Paddy. "It's only when they grow up and marry bikers that she kicks off."

Molly laughs and takes a swing at her husband. Fortunately for him he's well out of range.

"Hey guys, I really appreciate this. I'll ask Anna though. Sometimes she can be funny about going on her own to a new place."

Harley and Anna stomp down the stairs in a noisy clump of giggles and too-big rubber boots.

"Harley says we're going to visit his gran, Daddy. She's got goats and chickens and rabbits and all different animals. I get to wear my wellies 'cause of mud."

So much for Anna's being reluctant to go.

"You coming with us, Daddy?"

"No, sweetheart, not right now. Daddy's got to stay here and help out Paddy."

"Don't be silly. He's the one who does help with you. You don't do help with him."

"Your dad's doing help with some important writing," Paddy explains. "He's real good with writing, Anna. Me, I don't got the head for it."

"You being silly too. Peoples write with a pen, not their heads. Everyone knows that."

"Anna, your dad and Paddy will come out there first thing after lunch."

"Promise?"

"Cross my heart."

"And hope to die?"

"That too."

Molly has already packed two small backpacks. She picks them up and starts for the door.

"Come on you two. Don't want to keep those poor chickens waiting out in the rain do we?"

Anna stamps across the room in her oversized boots, reaches over and gives me a kiss.

"Bye, bye Daddy."

Then hand in hand the two children follow Molly.

"We gonna see chickens in the rain," sings Anna.

Harley joins in.

"Chickens in the rain, chickens in the rain! We're gonna see chickens in the rain."

Then they're gone, leaving a vapor trail of song behind them.

Sister Act 2

Paddy meets me outside the house as I roll back from the fish and chip shop with our lunch.

"Greenie, first thing to say, is that everyone is OK."

"Everyone?" I ask, panic rising in my gut.

"There's been some trespasser or intruder out at Gwen's place and she took a shot at him."

"Christ, Paddy! Sorry, man. Shooting? What kind of a shooting? The kids?"

It's the freaking Russians! They're on to us for sure if they followed Molly.

"Slow down now. I told you, no one's hurt, everyone's fine. Molly's phone was fading out. She said she'd explain it when we get there."

"Come on, man, let's go. Those bastards. Now, Paddy. Let's head out right now. Please. Also, as we go, you wanna make a call?"

"Who am I calling."

I shoot him with my index finger.

"I think it might be time, Paddy."

"I thought you been saying your family was peaceful clothes crooks, not shoot-'um-up gangsters."

"Now is not the time for fine distinctions, man. Can you get what we need or not?"

"I'll try, but Greenie, that's not all."

"What else you got for me. I mean I was gone, what,

fifteen minutes. How much trouble can boil up in fifteen minutes?"

"That woman's come back. You know, the posh London bird."

"Great timing."

She's all in black, including a small black pillbox hat with a veil flipped back over the top. As soon as I come through the door I am mowed down by a machine-gun volley of words blasting at me through a cloud of cigarette smoke.

"I've just come from Benjamin's funeral," she rants. "Some kind of woodland burial business. Real leafy eco-friendly kind of thing. But that was Ben, wasn't it just! Eco-friendly to the bitter end was Ben. Bitter end indeed. All those badly turned out disabled people there looking like refugees from some damn war or other. And a man dressed up as a woman! A Jew too, judging by the little round hat and the nose. Jesus, trust my brother to collect all the freaks. And the vicar, who I guess wasn't a proper vicar. One of those humanist people. Sounded like a vicar though. Without God or Jesus, of course. Damn man didn't really know Ben at all. You could tell. Then all that hippy music. No proper hymns or anything. Awful! Of course I didn't go on to the thing afterwards at Ben's house. The wake or whatever she called it. Anyway, why would I want to go there? That bloody woman, in my parents' house, like she owned it. I suppose she does own it. Although if I have my way, not for long. My son wanted to go. He really loved his uncle you see. I told him, 'You go if you want to Harry. Not me. Oh no, not me.' So I left him there. He can make his own way back to the station. It was all I could manage to do to be at the funeral with that damn woman."

All out of ammunition, she stopped suddenly.

"I expected to see you there, Mr. Green. Why ?"

"I wasn't invited. Like I told you, Mrs. Quest, I only met your brother that one time. We weren't friends. No reason for anyone to invite me. Listen. I'm sorry, but this is not a real good moment for me. Can we talk maybe tomorrow?"

"I'm not going to be here tomorrow, Mr. Green. I've got to get back to London this evening. My husband and I have a very important function."

"Well then, can we talk on the phone? It's just that something has happened and I need to deal with it. It's urgent, Mrs. Quest. Really urgent."

She leans forward, ignoring what I am saying to her

"Have you spoken to his friends, to that woman?"

She makes a sour face.

I am crazy to be with Anna. This damn woman is yacking at me so hard I can't think straight. I know the bastards are closing in. Maybe watching the house right now. Are they still out at Molly's mother's, waiting for me to come so they can gun down both of us? Will Paddy be able to get us guns?

"Mr. Green?"

"As I promised I would, yes I've talked to them. Can we please discuss this tomorrow, Mrs. Quest?"

"Mr. Green! Didn't I pay you a lot of money to do this for me?"

"Yeah, you did, but like I'm trying to tell you..."

She gives me an angry-eyed, overly-dramatic look of exasperation, stubs out her cigarette in a saucer on the floor and stands up, smoothing down her skirt .

"I've only myself to blame. My husband told me I was silly giving money to someone I didn't know, a person with no real experience in these matters, a person with a disability as well. I told him I thought you would be perfect for the job. You know what? He was right. I made a mistake. He's a barrister. I think I told you that before. Well, he knows people, and we'll be engaging a proper detective agency to look into this whole thing. Damn woman is not getting away with this, I can promise you. Should have done that from the beginning. So, if you will be so good as to return the money, I won't detain you any longer and you can get on to your 'urgent business'. Mr. Green?"

"I don't have your money right now, Mrs. Quest."

She looks around my living room, as if trying to figure out what I've spent it on.

"No money?"

I cannot believe this damn woman.

"That's right, no money. Can you imagine that?"

"I warn you, Mr. Green, you do not want to take that tone with me."

"The last time I looked, Mrs. Quest, this was my house. My house, shitty as it is, my tone whatever it is."

"Did I tell you my husband Oren is a barrister? Did I?"

She pulls a business card from her bag and slams it on the chair.

"You sure did. Maybe four or five times you told me."

"Well then. If you know what's good for you, you will either find the money and pay me back or you will be hearing from him in his professional capacity. Do I make myself clear."

"As a god-damned bell. If he wants to give me grief, your barrister husband will have to get himself at the end of the fucking line."

That feels better. Much better.

"Now if you'll excuse me, lady, I've got somewhere to go."

She moves quickly to the door and with perfect movie timing turns to offer a parting line.

"I suppose this is what I should have expected from a disabled person living on a council estate. And you're not even British."

"Amen to that, lady. Amen to that."

Leo the Late Bloomer

We pull in to a cement-covered yard, maybe fifty by a hundred feet. It separates the rambling one story house from a corrugated-sided barn. In one corner is an old tractor and scattered around are large pieces of rusting steel. Overlooking all of this are about a dozen massive steel sculptures, some thin twisted pillars like totem poles and others resemble soaring, wind-filled sails. Our arrival is met by the frenzied barking of two big red dogs that almost flip themselves over as they slam against the ends of chains attached to the barn.

"Everyone is fine," says Molly. "Well, everyone except for some dumb bloke carrying around a bum full of buckshot."

"Can't be sure about that," her mother says. "Could be it hit him somewheres else."

Molly's mother is wearing steel-toed boots and worn bib overalls on top of a white teeshirt. Apparently she's impervious to the sharp wind cutting through her yard. She's somewhere in her fifties and, like one of those Grapes of Wrath women photographed by Dorothea Lange - my dad was a big Grapes of Wrath fan - she is raw-boned gorgeous. Deep blue wide-set eyes and brown hair streaked with grey, worn in a heavy plait curled on the top of her head. Although slight, she has large hands, smoothly-muscled arms and the firm, restrained handshake of someone who is totally confident in their strength. Most striking, however, is her stillness.

185

"She's a sculptor," Paddy had told me as we drove out to the farm. "Does her stuff in metal. Real tough old lady is our Gwen. So, between her and Molly, you ain't got to be worrying about the kids."

Paddy's words had not reassured me, nor had his failure to make good on his offer of getting us guns, but seeing Gwen does. She looks as if she could chew on iron and spit out hot rivets.

"Nice to meet you, Anna's father."

"And nice to meet you too, Molly's mother."

She grins. Nice teeth. Lovely full lips. What the hell am I thinking here? This is Molly's mother, for Christ's sake. She must have at least twenty years on me. I've never been drawn to an older woman before. This is not the time to start. Reluctantly I pull my eyes away.

"I expect you want to see your daughter."

"Do they know what happened with, you know, the shooting and all that?" I ask.

"No, the bang woke them up, but we told them it was a piece of steel that fell over in the barn. They're inside playing. Just hang on a minute."

She turns to Paddy.

"I need to get a piece of plywood so your friend can get into the house. Come give me a hand."

The two of them go over to the barn and disappear inside.

"It was still dark, so didn't see him, but the dogs started barking," explains Molly. "Mum grabs the 12 gauge, thinking it's a fox that's been taking hens. She runs out across the yard and this guy knocks her over and the gun goes off. By the time I get there he's done a runner."

"So what you've just told me, that's it?"

"Yeah, more or less. Must have got hit though. Blood on the ground and a trail of it going out over that way."

She points to a field off to the left of the barn.

"Did you go after him?"

"Didn't want to leave the children. Now you and Paddy are here, we could go have a butchers, but I reckon he's long gone."

Paddy and Gwen put down the plywood and I wheel up the improvised ramp into the house. The two kids are sitting close together on a thick mustard-yellow rug looking at a book.

"Then one day," Anna reads out, "Leo bloomed!"

"Daddy!" she shouts, dropping the book and running over to me.

She climbs up in my lap. She puts her head against my chest. I stroke her hair.

"Hi, Pumpkin. How you doing?"

"Molly's mom's got dogs and chickens and rabbits and goats too and…".

"Slow down, little one."

"You come to take me and Harley home, Daddy? Please can we stay here just a little bit longer? Please."

"We'll see. Remember, you two have to go back to school the day after tomorrow."

"Daddy, please, please, please!"

"Come on you two," says Gwen. "Need some help feeding those chickens."

Anna and Harley jump up and rush to the door.

"Wellies," Gwen calls to them.

They flop down on the floor, pull on their rubber boots and dash outside.

I pick up Anna's book and begin to read.

'Leo couldn't do anything right.'

Goats and Whiskey

"So you've met Hedgy, have you?" says Gwen. "Our very own wild man. I've got lots of time for the old tranny yid."

Oh no. A friendly anti-Semite. Not her. Please, not her!

"Despite all that showman nonsense, he's the real article. Fine artist. Know him from the Art School. Used to teach there myself, until I packed it in a few years ago. Wanted more time for my own work. Shame what happened to Sarah. He worshiped the woman. I'm sure you saw that when you visited his studio. You an artist, Bob?"

"Me? No, I'm just a civilian."

"Are you now? Well civilian or not, my Molly says you're a decent chap, and she doesn't say that about many folk. You've got yourself a smashing little girl too. Lively and well behaved. Can't ask for more."

"She's something special, true enough."

I'm sitting with Gwen and the two children in front of a log fire. We're having hot chocolate and crumpets with honey. Until she came out with the yid remark, I was feeling warmer than I have in weeks. More than a hint of ice is now creeping back into my gut.

Outside the light is starting to fade. There's a blast of cold air, as the door opens and Molly and Paddy come in. Harley runs to his mother. He throws his arms around one of her pillar-like legs. She bends slightly and ruffles his hair.

"Any luck?" asks Gwen.

"Depends how you're wanting to define 'luck'," Molly replies.

"Maybe you two should come into the kitchen," Paddy says. "Harley. Anna. You wanna watch the telly?"

He doesn't have to ask twice. Harley grabs the remote control and they settle down a couple of feet from the screen. Surprisingly, neither Paddy nor Molly tell them, as they usually do, to move back. Something's not right.

After he's poured tea for everyone except me, I get the crap instant coffee, Paddy sits down, crosses his heavy arms across his chest and leans back. The chair squeals in protest. Gwen gives him a cool stare. Sheepishly he lets the chair ease forward until all four legs are grounded.

"Good news, no body," he says. "Bad news, a mess of blood."

"Where?" Gwen asks.

"Up at the copse" Molly says. "We followed the trail until we came across some fresh tyre tracks. Paddy reckons a lorry's been parked there. Can still see blood on the ground. Whoever if was, looks to be bleeding pretty badly."

"We have to call the police right away," Gwen says, getting up. "Should have done that first thing this morning."

"Mum," says Molly. "Wait with that call. We need to explain some things first."

"Right," Gwen says, after Paddy lays it all out for her,

including the Russian angle. "I'm sorry, but we've still got to call the police. It was an accident. If we don't call them and he goes to hospital, this whole thing becomes more of a mess than it already is."

"He's not going to tell anyone about what happened," I say. "If he had, the police would be here already. Besides, he'd have to explain what he was doing out here snooping around in the middle of the night."

Gwen gives me a thoughtful look then sits down and studies her sculptor's hands.

"Listen, Gwen, although I don't know who he was or what he was after, I reckon it's likely to be something to do with me, and I'm truly sorry to bring my troubles to your door. For that matter to your guys' door as well. So, I think it would be for the best, Paddy, if you gave me and Anna a lift back to the city. With all what's gone down, I figure it's time for us to pack up and move on. Whoever it is, he's got too damn close."

"And you were saying how I been watching too many films," Paddy says with a snort. "Next off you'll be telling us to leave you the last bullet and go on without you so you don't slow us down."

"Cute, Paddy, but I'm serious, man."

"You know, Greenie," says Molly, "I've been thinking. I figure the shooting probably doesn't have anything to do with you at all."

"How's that?" I ask.

"First off, there's no way anyone's going to know Anna or you are out here, leastways from one day to the next. Second, and more real, is your Russian mates aren't going to be driving a lorry, and by the tracks that was at least a two, maybe three ton job."

"Pikeys," Gwen says softly. "Of course."

"Mum!" Molly shouts.

"Oh, dear. Sorry Paddy. No offence intended."

"None taken."

"Pikeys?" I ask.

"Travellers," Gwen explains. "Paddy's parents were travellers, and they don't much appreciate being called pikeys. I should have thought of them straight off. About a week ago a group parked in a field not more than a few miles from here. Nothing they like better than a bit of scrap metal, and a place like this is like cow pats to flies. Poor man was probably just having a look see. I don't want a dead person on my conscience or a blood feud breaking out. I better drive over to make sure he's OK."

"Don't think that would be such a great idea," Paddy says. "Let me go first thing in the morning. Gwen, how many goats you got now?"

"Four. Why?"

"Assuming the bloke is still with us, we needs to offer up something. A horse would be favourite, but seeing as how you don't have one, I reckon a goat and a couple of bottles of whiskey would sort it. Now, if he's popped his clogs, we got us a whole other thing."

Goats, whiskey, whatever the hell it takes. What I don't need right now is another bunch of crazy people out gunning for me.

Absolutely Delicious

"**M**olly's father? A long time gone, Bob."

"As in passed away or…?"

"As in gone gone. Back to his mummy and daddy, back to his comfortable world."

We had real down-home dinner of spaghetti with clams and freshly baked bread. The kids are in bed. Paddy and Molly have gone out for a drink at a nearby pub. I've abandoned my wheelchair and we're sitting together on the couch in Gwen's living room drinking wine, watching the fire and exploring the past. Firelight softens the stark beauty in her face. The wine is helping too. I haven't felt so relaxed since I can't remember when. At least way before the Odessa Yids came to town.

"We were very young. Stupidly serious artists who were going to set the world on fire. Children did not figure in that particular conflagration. You know, kids were the thin end of the wedge. What followed, as night follows day, was getting married, being tied down, responsibilities, mortgages, having to make money, all that stuffy bourgeois shit. So, as soon as he knows I've got a bun in the oven, he runs off. The boy never did manage to set the world alight. Instead he ends up being tied down and up to his elegant Jewish neck in plastic-covered three-piece suites, working at his father's furniture shop in Golders Green. Me, the crazy, bad-influence shiksa, 'who thank God our Marty escaped from', was left holding the baby."

That's good. I was being too thin skinned when she made that crack about Hedgy.

"So Molly is half Jewish?"

"Yep, but as you well know, Bob, the half she's got doesn't count. Then she meets up with Paddy and finds Jesus Christ. Strange the way things work out, isn't it?"

"Sure is. Her father ever have anything to do with her?"

"Yeah, a couple of times after she was born he came by but pretty soon less and less. Then one day a mutual friend told me he'd gotten married. Haven't seen him since. Yeah. Within a few years he had a brood of kosher kiddies. End of story. "

"Wonder what he'd think if he saw her now."

"Probably the same thing you're thinking, Bob. Oh, yeah, I know I've heard it before. Too many damn times before."

"Hang on now, I didn't say a word. I love the woman. Really. If it weren't for her and Paddy, I don't know where I'd be. They've come through big time. So…".

"Yeah, sorry. I'm being too defensive. No reason for it. Anyhow, Molly went her own way. Which is the way it should be. Am I right?"

Reaching over, she snags the bottle and pours us both another glass.

"Right. Absolutely."

"She went off to read American Literature but didn't care much for the university types. Can't blame her. Never took to those smug, self-important bastards myself. Met Paddy at a Richard Thompson gig. You've heard of him, right?"

"No, doesn't ring a bell. He English?"

"Yes, very. Anyway, their meeting was almost like in the song, which you'll also not know, so I won't bore you with explaining. As these stories go, they met, he fell in love with her, she fell in love with him and with bikes and all that goes with it, including the tattooing. That's the artistic genes. What with that and Paddy doing up bikes, the two of them do alright."

She grins and takes a long pull at her wine. I think we're on the second, maybe the third bottle. Who's counting? Obviously not me.

"I always thought I was broadminded, you know. Could be everyone thinks they're broadminded. Ever hear anyone say, 'I'm narrow minded'? Course you haven't. But I was an artist, I am an artist, and a real artist shouldn't be, couldn't be shocked. Surprised. Yes, surprised. Sure. But never shocked. You know what? That's total bloody nonsense. Really is, total bloody nonsense. When she brought Paddy here for the first time, riding in on the back of his motorcycle, leathered and tattooed and all, I was surprised, but more than that, I was shocked. Really out and out shocked. Me, the artist. Ha!"

"The next shock, a whole lot easier to come to terms with, was what a lovely, decent, caring person she'd found. Even with Jesus, or as Paddy would say, because of Jesus. That man would do anything for my Molly, anything at all."

She gathers her legs under her, reaches across and takes my hand. She turns it over and traces a finger across the calluses on my palm and inside of my fingers.

"From pushing that damn contraption. Even with gloves on they get like that."

"So what about that, Bob?"

I am finding her exploratory touch frighteningly erotic. A cripple and an older woman. Even a very beautiful older woman. A grandmother for Christ's sake! This cannot be happening. I do not pull away. There are three empty wine bottles lined up on the floor. I think we've both got a load on.

"I've heard all about the Russians and what happened, but what happened to you?" she asks, pointing to the empty wheelchair.

I shake my head.

"Some kind of Chinese thing. Can't remember what it's called, but the quacks say I may get the legs back, but it's pretty much a long shot."

"Not promising?"

"Not very. I'm just trying to figure out how to make it through each day and from one day to the next. But, hey, it could be a lot, lot worse. I've seen a lot worse."

"Still, it must be difficult for you and for Anna."

We're now officially holding hands. After a couple of feeling-her-way minutes, she slides over, takes the captive hand and with it carries my arm around her shoulder and then cuddles into me.

"This is cozy," she says. "You comfortable?"

"Very."

"That's good."

"Very."

With her sculptor-strong hands she pulls my face down gently towards her. She tastes of garlic and oregano and red wine and olives and, most curiously, of desert-dry heat.

Simple Nobility

"You sure you're up for this, Greenie? No telling what might kick off."

"No sweat, man. When am I going to get another chance to see real gypsies."

"Travellers, not gypsies. Gypsies are a whole different lot. Come from somewheres in Eastern Europe. These people are home grown or maybe Irish."

"Gotcha. Travellers."

"You OK? Look like shit, you do."

"Too much to drink last night. Haven't had a hangover like this for years."

Paddy says nothing about seeing me rolling out of Gwen's room this morning. When I woke up she was already at work in the barn. From the kitchen window I could see red sparks bouncing and scattering out into the yard.

"Get this coffee down you and we'll get going."

I am still trying to figure out why what happened, happened. Was it a charity thing for a poor, displaced cripple? Was it the wine? Thinking back, I can't say for sure if anything did happen. I was drunk, too drunk, and she was matching me glass for glass. Most likely we both passed out. So why did I wake up without any clothes on?

"You ready, Greenie?"

"Yeah, let's do it. What about the kids?"

"Off out for a walk with Molly."

I slide into the passenger seat. Paddy loads my wheelchair in the back with the goat. Christ, but the damn thing stinks to high heaven!

It takes no more than ten or fifteen minutes before we find the travellers. Despite Paddy's explanation, I was still expecting painted horse-drawn carts, swarthy men with swarthy smiles and guitars, girls in billowy blouses. No such luck. Instead of a romantic movie set, there are half a dozen big trailer homes scattered about and an assortment of trucks and cars. Washing is hung out on clothes lines. Kids are running here and there. On the far side of the muddy field a few horses are tethered. A load of junk is piled near the entrance to the site. We drive in. The van bucks and thumps across the uneven ground. The goat bleats in protest. I bet the damn beast has crapped all over my chair.

"I'm sure you won't, but don't say anything. OK?"

"Whatever."

We pull up in front of one of the trailers. A middle-aged women stands in the doorway, her enormous arms folded. As Paddy brings out my chair, two wide-faced men wearing scowls approach us. I hoist myself into the chair. I can't tell if it is covered in goat shit. It doesn't smell too good.

"What you want here?" asks one of the men.

Four other men begin to stroll over, together with a mob of curious kids. The doorway of each trailer is now occupied by women with folded arms and hostile stares. This does not look promising.

"Come to talk," Paddy says. "Come to make the peace."

"Oh, yeah," replies the man closest to us.

He's wearing red suspenders, a flat hat and very muddy boots. His broad face is laced with red veins. He looks extremely pissed off.

"Didn't know we was at war," he says, turning his head to the side and projectile spitting a load of what must be tobacco juice into the mud.

Paddy says something that I can't understand.

The man looks surprised. He returns the words, while weighing up the barbarian biker. They begin to speak in a mixture of English and whatever the hell the other language is. As they do, tension begins to drain away. Smiles break out. Paddy opens the van door and produces a bottle of whiskey. The man calls over one of the kids, who is sent off and returns a few minutes later with some glass jars. Whiskey is poured for all the men. I'm left out, which is fine by me. It is 9:30 in the morning. All the men tip up their jars and mutter an incomprehensible benediction.

After some more chatter, Paddy brings out the goat and hands the rope to the tobacco spitter, who then yells something to one of the trailer-door women. Some moments later a scrawny teenage boy steps out. His head and one of his hands is bandaged. Eyes focused on the ground, he slowly walks over to where we are. The man says something to him and he nods, still keeping his eyes averted. Paddy says something. More nods. Then the man spits in his hand and Paddy spits in his. They shake.

I'm watching an ancient ritual that, with a shot of romantic imagination, seems to lift the entire encounter up from the muddy field to a more majestic place.

"What was all that about?" I ask when we're on the road back to Gwen's place.

"Clearing the air is all. What needed doing. Gwen can sleep easy now. She'll have no more midnight callers, at least from that lot."

My dad would have loved this guy. He was always talking about how you could find a simple nobility of spirit in the most unlikely of people. My friend Paddy is about as unlikely as can be.

Scars

"And these?" I ask Gwen, touching the cluster of dimpled scars on the side of her thigh.

"Welding burns. Stupid really. They told me to get protective coveralls, but I didn't pay attention. I'm lucky not to have more. In fact, I do have a couple more."

She takes my hand and presses it against her right breast. I feel the thin hard ridge raised slightly above her soft flesh. I'd noticed it, but being guided there is very different, an intimate gesture of vulnerability.

Brought up on a California diet of female perfection, natural or, more usually, air brushed and surgically enhanced, I had come to expect it. I am discovering what I've missed, as well as the reason for beauty marks.

"Why welding and steel? Looks heavy, dangerous stuff. I wouldn't have figured that for an obvious choice."

"You mean for a woman?"

"Ah, not really."

"Come on, Bob. Not much problem reading between those lines. I've heard it all before. Watercolours. My art school tutor actually said that. Bloody watercolours! Calder, David Smith, Caro, Hepworth, Moore, that's what I wanted. Loved what they did. I could give you all kinds of art-crit-shit reasons, but when you get past all that, for me it comes down to a visceral thing. If it's right, I know in my gut it's right. You know, for most people steel is intractable. It isn't at all. Melt it, cut it, weld it so you make the piece define its own space. Softer than wood or marble to work with. That's what I love about it. You can push the steel, push it to precisely where you want it to go."

"So, what about you and me, where do we go."

"You and me? From here? Please, Bob, you're a lovely boy, but I'm old enough to be your mother."

"So?"

"So, my dear boy. That means, besides all the obvious Oedipal stuff, from here you go back to Norwich, and from here, I go back to my work."

"Oh, I see. Yeah."

"You thought we were going to be an item, didn't you? Hey, don't look like that. This was lovely, really it was, but I'm not going to get involved with you, or for that matter anyone else. I'm not up for compromise about how I live my life. Besides," she laughs, "could you imagine introducing me to your parents? Come on now. Christ all mighty, they're probably younger than I am."

"That wouldn't have been a problem, Gwen. They're both dead."

"Oh, I am so sorry, Bob. Stupid of me."

"It's OK. How were you to know? My dad, he died a couple of years ago. I never knew my mother. She died when I was about one. Cancer."

She strokes the back of my neck.

"Can I at least see you again?"

"Of course you can. I'd like that very much, as long as we agree on the ground rules."

"Which are?"

"No commitments, no promises and no long faces, especially no long faces."

She pulls me too her and kisses me softly on the mouth.

"There," she says. "Come on, it's late and I've got animals to look after."

She gets out of bed, throws on a blue terrycloth robe and goes out of the room.

I wish she hadn't kissed me like that.

The Last One Rolling

A few hours after we got back to Norwich, Molly brought over the evening paper.

"Sorry to be the one to tell you, Greenie, but I think this story here is about one of your disabled friends."

'The body, identified as that of Martin Saunders, a local disabled man, has been found at the bottom of an elevator shaft in his apartment building. One of his neighbours called the police after hearing a scream and finding the elevator doors opening and closing on an open, empty shaft. The police are investigating. They have asked for witnesses.'

Not long after, Hedgy, Sylvia and I, together with Henry and Paddy, and, of course, Norman, are sitting in the living room of Brendan's Oak Street apartment. It's a small room, something like ten by fifteen. Yellow leatherette couch and two matching chairs, a modern wooden sideboard, a few landscape prints, a large television set and a red-green, swirly-patterned carpet. It's a squeeze and stuffy, but no one seems to mind. The atmosphere is so down-in-the-mouth that no one has even offered to make a cup of tea. That's the upside. The downside is that everyone is gloomily lost in their own thoughts. Even Norman, lying there, large head between his paws, looks deathly sad. It's Brendan who finally breaks the funereal quiet.

"Poor Martin. Escaped from the bloody care home, survived a mugging and then… Bloody Nora but life ain't fair! Poor Martin. Damn."

Something heavy slams into the front door. Everyone looks up startled. Once more there is a rammed thud. Henry gets up, steps across and throws the door open.

Sitting strapped up and ramrod straight in his electric wheelchair, Ronald 'Bomber' Burns rolls into the room. As far as I can tell, he can only move his eyes and the fingers of his right hand.

"Sorry," he says. "Didn't know you were having a party. Oh, hello there, Bob Green. Didn't know you hung out with this rabble."

"I…".

"No party, Ronald," Brendan cuts me off, "a meeting is what this 'rabble' is having. So, what can we do for you?"

"It's more about what I can do for you, Brendan."

"Really? Well, I guess there's a first time for everything."

"Yeah. OK. I hear you. I know we've had our differences, but when I heard about what happened to Martin Saunders, coming on top of all the other recent deaths, I thought maybe you lot could use some assistance, like proper military assistance."

"Are you serious?" Brendan asks. "Who the hell do you propose we invade, Bomber?"

"Very funny, Brendan. But ask yourself, do any of you have experience with violence, especially orchestrated violence? Didn't think so. Well, I do have experience. Lots of experience."

"I thought you didn't approve of what the Rollers were

206

doing," Hedgy says.

He is suitably dressed for a wake. Black flats and tights, a modest scoop-neck dress, also black, subdued makeup, no jewellery and all topped off by his pageboy wig. As he is sitting, I can see that he's wearing his yarmulke. God forbid he should start saying kaddish.

"That's dead right, I don't approve, Daisy," replies Ronald. "But what I approve of even less, is people being killed off just for sticking their heads above the parapet."

"So," Brendan says, "you saying you think we should be going to war?"

"Not at all, Brendan. No. I think you're already in the middle of a bloody war and to be honest, you're losing it."

"And you're proposing what?" I ask.

"That you let me help you to plan a defensive strategy. After all, Brendan, as far as I can tell, you're the last of the so-called Rolling Dervishes."

"He is," Hedgy says. "The last bloody one."

"So am I in or what?" Ronald asks.

Brendan looks around the room. Hedgy nods his agreement.

"Why not," I say.

"Sylvia?"

"Up to you, Brendan," she responds.

"OK, Bomber," Brendan says. "Personally, I'm not convinced. However, seems I am outvoted, so you're in."

"Wise decision," Ronald says with a triumphant smirk. "So first things first. You got any idea who the enemy is?"

Brendan lays out the list of potential candidates.

"Christ!" Ronald exclaims. "So it could be any of them?"

"Or maybe someone we haven't figured," I add.

I glance over at Brendan. I think he shakes his head for a 'no', meaning, I assume, if it's not some random spastic twitch, that he hasn't told the others about the police reports and doesn't want me to say anything.

"Well, if you boys won't, I will, "Sylvia says. "First thing in the morning I'm off to Bethel Street. I don't care if we don't have the evidence. What we do have is a lot of people with motives. We can at least give them that to work with. The Evening News would love that story as well. Something like, 'Murderer of Disabled People Stalks the City'."

"I'm glad someone is finding a silver lining to this particular cloud. Nothing like being able to make a name for yourself and make money from the ill fortune of your friends."

"Bravo, Hedgy," Brendan calls out. "Took you no time at all to replace Martin as your target for verbal abuse. How about making faces at Sylvia?"

"At least I can make a face when I want to, Brendan."

"Time out!" I shout so loud that Norman leaps up and begins to bark.

"Norman, down!"

"You guys are completely nuts. There is a crazed wheelchair killer out there and the best you can do is …".

"Not actually a wheelchair killer, Bob. No, no one is

out there killing wheelchairs. It's the people who use the wheelchairs who are being killed."

"Thanks for that helpful correction, Hedgy, but let's cut to the chase, shall we. For me, right now, right this minute, the most important question is 'What about Brendan?' "

"Me?"

"Yeah, you. Don't you think you're going to need protecting? You're the last trophy, the last head missing from the wall."

"That's nice. Thank you, Bob"

"He's right, you know," Ronald chips in.

"Morris and I will hang with you 24/7, Brendan, until the cops nail the bumbaclot who's doing this."

"I can get some of the boys around as well," Paddy offers.

"Which boys?" Hedgy asks.

"A few bikers I know. Nothing they likes better than a bit of a ruck."

"Need to set up a defensive perimeter," Ronald says. "First rule is secure your base before venturing out to engage the enemy."

"Hey, just wait!" Brendan yells, arms windmilling in anger or frustration or both. "How about what I want? Don't want to be surrounded by lot of people looking out for me, telling me where I can go, where I can't go, what I should do and what I shouldn't. I've been disabled all my life, and had to fight long and fight hard for my independence. I am not about to let some murdering coward take it away! "

"Is a little loss of independence, just for a while, worse than the alternative?" Sylvia observes. "Must be practical, Brendan."

"If I wanted to be practical, Sylvia, I would have stayed locked up in that bloody care home in Kent, watching my life dribble away. That would have been practical and safe, but it would have been a one-little-death-a-day kinda safe. The hell with that."

Beans Spilt

"I didn't have your phone number, Bob, but you told me you lived on Pilling Park Road, so I've been going from door to door. Didn't take too many doors before someone told me where the American lived who used a wheelchair. Hope you don't mind."

If I had? Too late. Delia Castle has found me. She has completely lost her post-Legless-Ben glamour. The makeup gone, the shapelessness returned. Even the spark in her eyes has dimmed.

"I saw the report in the paper about Martin. I am so, so sorry about that. He had a foul mouth, but really wasn't a bad little man, was he? I am so sorry about what happened."

"You've come up here and knocked on all those doors to tell me that?"

"Sort of, yes. I have more though, more to tell you."

She fixes her eyes on the wall behind me. Outside I hear Anna, Harley and some of the other neighborhood kids screaming and shouting. Only two weeks until Christmas. Only a few more days of school before the hysteria begins to build for real.

"I don't know, Bob, don't know where to begin."

She lapses into silence.

"Sylvia. Let me start with Sylvia."

"Sylvia? Why Sylvia?"

"Just wait, I'll explain. She phoned earlier today.

Haven't spoken to her since Ben's funeral. We were always quite close, you see, being carers and all that. She told me she had gone to the police with these suspicions about what had happened to Ben and the others. Said she got brushed off and wanted to know what I thought."

"And?"

"And I told her I thought it sounded crazy, pretty farfetched."

"I see. So, why tell me?"

"Because it isn't so farfetched."

"No? You could have told Sylvia that."

"Yes, I could have. I didn't though. She's a friend, you see."

"And I'm not."

"That's right, Bob, you're not. Also, after I spoke to her, I started thinking about everything and for some reason thought I could talk to you, seeing as you're sort of involved and sort of not involved."

"I'm having a hard time with this, Delia."

She picks nervously at the arm of the easy chair.

"Ben. Let me tell you about Ben first. You know, most of the time when we were at home, he was often very sweet, even considerate. But when we were out he could be downright unpleasant to me, almost as if he enjoyed embarrassing me in front of other people. Remember how he was that night in the pub before he … Remember? Well, one time, not all that long ago, we were at the Theatre Royal, a play by one of the few people he could abide, Alan Bleasdale or David Edgar, some left winger like that. Anyway, during the intermission he started going on at me about something. We quarreled and in the end I left him there and started for home. I had to do that quite a lot. That's when I met Maurice. Remember, I introduced him to you at Starbucks? Well, he was very kind, said he could see I was upset and did I want to go for a drink. That's when it started, although they had actually already started before me."

She stops abruptly and looks around the room as if she is surprised to find herself here.

"Bob?"

"Right here, Delia."

She stares at me. I think she's trying to convince herself I can be trusted, but her eyes are more lifeless than inquisitive.

"He asked me, Maurice did, if Ben was always like that with me. He said that no one should have to put up with such abusive behaviour. Then he told me he had had similar problems and asked if I would like to come along to a meeting with him and a few likeminded people who had got together to support each other."

"A mutual support group kinda deal?"

"Yes, I suppose you could call it that. Sure. A support group."

"Would you like a cup of coffee, Delia?"

"Do you have tea? Thanks. Milk, no sugar."

I roll into the kitchen. She follows me. I fill the kettle.

"I met them a week or so later at Maurice's house out

at Hingham. Five of them were there. With me, six." She stops abruptly. "No. I can't. No."

The kettle is whistling. She gets up and begins to pace.

"I don't know how to stop it. So you're going to have to do it. Can you do it? Can you stop it? Stop it now?

"Slow down. Stop what?"

"The accidents, stop the accidents. I thought Ben was the last, but no, now they're saying they want more. Martin is just the first. They want Brendan and even you. That's right, they want you too, Bob. I really liked Brendan. He was always so very kind to me. I tried to tell them enough was enough, and I thought they had agreed we were finished. Now Martin is dead. So obviously they didn't listen."

"So Ben was right after all, there was a list. Who, Delia? Who is doing the killing?"

"Who? Not sure. At least before Barry died, I'm not."

"What the hell do you mean, 'not sure'? Somebody is pulling the trigger."

"It's not like that, Bob. No, not simple like that. It's a kind of reciprocal arrangement. I made the phone call to Barry's district nurses. They didn't tell me exactly what would happen. Believe me they didn't. I found out later, after he died, that someone else fixed the alarm. Probably David Yallop. He's some kind of radio-controlled airplane geek. In exchange, one of the others did for Ben. I never knew who. Maurice said it would be safer that way, in case anyone thought they weren't genuine accidents. Then the only one who would not have an alibi was the person who would never be suspected."

"You still haven't told me who these people are. There's also the question of why. Why murder handicapped people?"

"Disabled people, Bob. Please."

"Wait a second. You're telling me that you are part of a group of psychos who have gone on a free-fire-zone murder spree, and you're worried about my fucking language!"

"Silly of me, Bob, I know. Old habits die hard."

"Yeah, harder than disabled people, I guess. You going to tell me who these people are or not?"

She picks up her cup, looks into it as if there was an answer swimming around in the tea and then, still searching, she puts it back on the table.

"Maurice. I told you about Maurice. He said most disabled people were little more than a burden on themselves and the rest of us too. Scroungers he called them, useless scroungers. Already half dead anyway, so …".

"His last name wouldn't be Piper, would it? The architect?"

From studiously trying to decode the mystery of the tea, her head snaps up in surprise.

"Yes. How did you know?"

"The name has come up, that's all. The others?"

"The man from the Centre, Mr. Yallop. I mentioned him before. Then two brothers called Gaines. Can't remember their Christian names."

She pauses, appearing to be struggling.

So assuming the Brothers Gaines are the sons of the people from the rest home, all the guesses about the identity of the murderers were right on the money. Imagine that.

"You said there were five. Who was the other one?"

"Yeah, five. Sorry. Motes. He was the fifth. That was Maurice's cousin, a priest named H. Motes. Everyone has their own reasons, but only Motes really talked about his in any great detail, although it never made much sense to me or, as far as I could tell, anyone else. Keeps talking about a Saint William and how he had been denied by the Church and forgotten because disabled people wouldn't come to him, wouldn't embrace his message. A bit around the twist is H. Motes. Said disabled people must be punished for their apostasy."

"Apostrophe?"

"No, no 'apostasy', not 'apostrophe'."

"Oh."

"That's OK. I had look it up myself. Something about renouncing religion."

"He laid that shit on me a couple of times. Finally had to tell him to piss off. Crazy old Motes. And here's me thinking he was a harmless nutcase."

"Will you, Bob? Will you stop them?"

"How do you think I would go about that, Delia? No way. You've got to take this to the cops."

"I thought about that, of course I did. But I don't want to go to jail, Bob."

"I don't see how you're going to duck that one. But if you lay it all out for them, it's more likely they'll go easy on you. There's also the abuse you suffered to weigh in the balance."

"I don't know."

"Listen, if it makes it any easier, I'll go with you. Do you have a lawyer?"

"I do, but I'm not sure he does this kind of thing."

"Call him. Have him or someone he recommends come with you tomorrow."

"I don't know. It's so bloody complicated. I tell myself I didn't do that to Ben. It was someone else. But when I think about it, and recently I have been thinking about it more and more. I did kill him. I did push him into the river. I've been having a nightmare, over and over. More like vision. It seems so real. It's always the same. I am standing by the river. I am watching myself on the other side pushing Ben down the slope. He's not resisting at all. Just slumped in his wheelchair, asleep or dead drunk. I don't see him go in, but I hear a loud splash, then a scream. The scream is me. It wakes me up. I've not been getting much sleep, you see. I am so tired, Bob. So bloody tired."

"Delia, if you want all this to stop, you have to tell the police."

"Tell the police. Yes," she sighs deeply. "You're right. Should have done that before it got this far."

"So, I'll meet you at the police station?"

She stares at me without seeing me.

"I'll meet you at the police station," she repeats robot like.

"11:00?"

"11:00."

She stands up.

"Don't you want to finish your tea?"

She doesn't answer, instead she sleepwalks across the floor, through the living room, opens the front door and goes out without closing it. I roll in pursuit and just catch a glimpse of her as she walks leaden-footed up the road.

Waiting for Delia

"Thanks for comIng along, Sylvia. Delia said she'd be here at 11:00. Should be arriving any time now."

We're sitting in the reception area in the police station.

"After the brush off I was given on Tuesday when I told Detective Sergeant Richards who we suspected, I am anxious to hear what he says when Delia tells her story. Have you told the others?"

"Not yet. Thought I'd wait to hear what the cops have to say."

"This is really great news, Bob. Literally. I've already drafted an article. Once we've spoken to the police I'll be ready to go with it. What a marvellous scoop!"

"I figured the 'great news' is that Brendan and I might not now be murdered."

"Oh, of course, that too."

Hedgy was dead right about this woman. Blind in more ways than one.

"It's ten after, Bob. You don't think she got cold feet?"

Before I can answer, Richards comes into reception. I don't recognize him at first. He has abandoned his combover and fully embraced his true, essential baldness. Without hair, his eyebrows stand out more, two startled, hump-backed caterpillars facing each other on an ice flow.

"Good morning. Would you like to come this way?"

We're taken along a narrow corridor to the same cheery interview room I was in before. At least Sylvia will not have to suffer the sight of this windowless hole. Richards places her hand on the back of a chair. She sits without hesitation. No unsure perching for this one. Norman folds up at her feet.

"We're waiting for Delia Castle," I begin. "She has some extremely important information about the series of accidents".

"Mr. Green," Richards interrupts, face mournful, caterpillars laying flat. "I'm afraid Mrs. Castle will not be joining us this morning."

"Well, I mean, yesterday afternoon she told me for sure she would be coming."

"I'm sorry to have to tell you, Mr. Green, Miss Banning, but Mrs. Castle was found dead at her home this morning."

Sylvia looses a loud gasp. Norman growls. Me? I feel a ball of ice settle in my chest.

"Her cleaning lady found her when she went in this morning. Again, I am sorry to be the bearer of such bad news. I can see this has clearly come as a terrible shock for you both. Can I get you a cup of tea?"

Cup of tea! Cup of fucking tea! What is the matter with these people? Sorry, Dad. But a person can take only so much before the crust of civilized behavior busts wide open and the 'effing', as Paddy called it, escapes.

After what I gauge as a suitable pause after hearing of a sudden death, I ask, "How did she die?"

"Although not official, and definitely not for publication, I can tell you that our initial finding is probable suicide."

Thinking back on what she told me last night and how defeated she seemed, suicide should maybe not be such a surprise.

"A note." Sylvia says, "Then you must have found a note."

"I can't comment on that, Miss Banning."

"If there was a note," I jump in, "I'm sure it will back up what we've come to tell you."

"Do you mind?" he says, reaching over to turn on a cassette recorder. "Alright, Mr. Green, if you feel you are able, go ahead, please."

I lay out how the suspicions Sylvia had brought to him before were confirmed by Delia's story about Maurice Piper and his friends. When I finish, Richards, who throughout has been studying me intently over prayerfully peaked hands, unpeaks them to reach over and turn off the recorder.

"Miss Banning. Mr. Green. What I am about to tell you, I am only telling you in strictest confidence. Miss Banning?"

Sylvia hesitates a few beats. "Of course," she says.

"First, and again this is strictly off the record, when we spoke the other day, Miss Banning, although I told you that without at least some specific evidence we could not proceed, I had had my own doubts as to whether the series of accidents experienced by disabled people were in fact unconnected or indeed accidents. Secondly, after listening to your accounts, I feel I can inform you both that Mrs. Castle did in fact leave a note."

He pauses, watching me. I smile thinly, not wanting, under the circumstances, to seem too pleased with myself.

"A suicide note. Well, then you will know what we are telling you is true."

"No, Mr. Green. I'm afraid not. It appears, at least according to the contents of her note, that the late Mrs. Castle took her life because she was filled with remorse over having pushed her husband into the Wensum. She makes no mention at all of the story you've just told me. Absolutely none."

Richards regards me quizzically, expecting a reply. Stunned by having vindication slapped away so unexpectedly, I find no words.

"Mr Green?" he says.

"Murder," is all I manage to get out.

"Mr. Green?"

"Not suicide. Murder. Why would she tell me such a fancy-assed story and then kill herself and leave a note like that? It doesn't make sense. Someone was trying to shut her up. It's obvious as the day is long."

Richards has got that look people put on when they're humoring UFO-abduction nuts

"That is a very serious allegation, Mr. Green. Let's look at this another way, shall we? Don't you see how your account is rather too conveniently close to the unsubstantiated story brought to me by Miss Banning? Could you not have possibly suggested this to Mrs. Castle, obviously a woman under severe stress, and she found it easy to fill in the rest? After all, that would be a lot easier than owning up to murdering her own husband, to actually pushing him into the river."

"Why the hell would I want to do that? "

He smiles thinly and gives me what I can only describe as an exaggerated Yiddishe shrug.

There's a whole lot more to this newly-bald mother than I had imagined.

Angels from Hell

I'm putting on my coat, ready to go out and catch the bus into the city. Sylvia and I are meeting the others at Hedgy's to tell them what went down at the police station. I reach for the door handle. There's a soft knock at the back door. No one knocks at the back door. I roll through the kitchen, picking up my cricket bat on the way.

"Hey, Greenie. You in there, mate?"

I lean the bat against the sink, reach up, throw the two bolts, undo the deadlock and open the door.

"Paddy, why the backdoor knock, man?"

"I think you may have yourself a bit of bother, mate."

""Bother seems to be my middle name, maybe my first name and my last name as well. So, what this time?"

"There's a bloke in a car across the road checking out the house."

"Are you sure about that, Paddy?"

"As sure as I'm standing here, Greenie."

"What's he look like."

"Young, maybe mid-20s. Couldn't see much else, him being sat in the car like he was. Looked good size though. Big head, wide shoulders."

"Great. Just watching, you say?"

"Far as I could tell."

I roll towards the front window. Paddy grabs my arm and stops me.

224

"Not a good idea. Once he sees that curtain twitching, he'll be off like a rat up a drainpipe. Then you'll never know who he is or why he's out there watching the house."

"How am I going to know anyway? It could be some guy eyeballing another house. Jealous boyfriend or husband. What makes you think he's watching me?"

"I came around the corner just as you was rolling up the ramp. I was there behind him and seen him taking pictures with one of those big-lens cameras."

"Well someone has found me for sure. Big guy, you say?"

Paddy nods.

"Think he's still out there?"

"Could be. Tell you what. I'll pop out the back, go to my place and take a butchers. Hang on here for a few minutes. Don't panic."

Easy for Paddy to say.

If I wasn't stuck in this damn chair I could go out the back door and take off. Still, if the bastard knows I'm here, he'll hang on or call for help or let some other hitter know where I am. What if he's already called?

Why photos? Why not just pick me off? Silenced long gun. By the time anyone figured out I'd been shot - assassination not being an everyday thing in Norwich - he'd be gone. Disappeared. Message delivered in public. Then he calls the cops and tells them I'm really Bobby Fishbaum, not Robert Green. That I'm in the country on a phony passport. Then the lovely Annabel Garanday has her story. Won't take long before the LA Times picks it up off the Net. And then... Then I'll be too dead to care. What about Anna though?

I hear the back door open.

"Yeah, bloke is still sitting out there. You want me to sort it out?"

Dangling from his hand is a mean-looking, rusty lug wrench.

"Jesus!"

He gives me a hard stare.

"Sorry, man. I'm sorta rattled here."

"I know," he says, offering up a Christian-forgiveness smile.

"Exactly what did you have in mind?"

"Oh, nothing too bloody. Thought I'd tap on his window and ask him over for a cuppa."

"Right. Are you shitting me, Paddy? A cup of tea? That's gotta be a real killer offer. Besides, for all you know he's packing."

"Packing?" he laughs. "What are you on about?"

"A gun, packing a gun."

"Let's not go there. Besides, I'll be real careful, real polite too."

"I don't know, man. Sounds a risky call."

"You gotta better idea, Greenie? If so, just let me know."

"No. I got nothing. If I was back home, I'd make a call. But here, I've got no backup."

"Me. You got me. And I've made a call."

"Who to?"

"Backup. We only need to wait about ten minutes or so."

"Thanks, but I don't want to drop you in the shit."

"Too late. We got what we got. OK?"

"A cup of tea?"

"A cup of tea," he laughs. "It's bloody cold out there. It's an offer he won't refuse. Trust me."

Five minutes later and I hear the throaty roar of a motorcycle. Then another and another.

Paddy goes to the front door and steps out, smacking the lug wrench against the palm of his hand. I roll behind him until I can see outside.

About twenty yards away a grey car is parked on the other side of the road surrounded by three large motorcycles, ridden by three large, leathered riders. One of them has opened the driver's door and is reaching in.

I stay in the house while Paddy crosses the road.

A few minutes later a very frightened looking guy, wearing shoes that look far too classy for his badly-cut, off-the-peg suit, stumbles in through the door. He's followed by Paddy and two tattooed hulks.

"You wanna put on the kettle, Greenie? I promised Mr. Jeffries here that cuppa."

Nice Cup of Tea

Mr. Jeffries cradles his mug of tea in his hands as if it linked him to a safer reality. He is a big, bulky guy, with a white-blond 50s flattop and a badly set nose. In other company he might just manage to look like a tough guy, but sitting here with Paddy and his Hell's Angels friends standing around him he looks to be a harmless, suitably cowed normal citizen.

"Like I told these gentlemen here, Mr. Green, I'm with the DWP. Department of Work and Pensions. I check to make sure people aren't making false claims."

"Yeah, he's telling the truth, Greenie. Look at this," Paddy says, passing me a plastic-coated identity card.

In the photo he appears cheerily confident, as if his ID would give him license and authority. Hunched over a chipped mug in my sparsely furnished living room, he looks neither cheery nor confident. He looks scared shitless. That's the general idea.

I've been here before. Me sitting where Jeffries is. Two Russian heavies, who stank of stale sweat and cloves, snatched me off the street as I was coming out of Cantor's after my, in retrospect too-regular, Tuesday night 3:00AM lox and eggs. They drove me to a warehouse somewhere in the Valley, where I was dropped into a hard folding chair and informed that my business was now their business. If that had happened to my grandfather, the one who worked for Bugsy Siegel and Mickey Cohen at the Flamingo in Vegas, there would have been a war. I didn't have the troops or, quite frankly, the balls. Stupidly, I went to the cops.

"It's routine, Mr. Green. I've never had any trouble before now. Routine, like I say."

"Hey, listen. No trouble, pal," I reply. "Don't worry about it. You like the tea?"

"Tea's fine. Thank you very much."

"You've got to see it from my side. Somebody watching my place and taking pictures, what am I supposed to make of that?"

"Sure," he says. "I understand, and now if I could have my phone back, and my camera, I'll get myself back to the office. They'll be wondering where I've got to."

He puts the half-finished cup on the floor, straightens his tie and starts to get up from the chair. Paddy drops a hand on his shoulder. Jeffries looks up at him, startled.

"Please, Mr. Green," he says in a plaintive voice. "I don't want any trouble. I'm only doing my job."

"I know you are. Hey, Paddy, go on, give this guy back his cell and his camera."

Paddy gestures to one of the others. He smiles, puts a many-ringed hand in his jacket pocket and gives a cellphone to Paddy, who passes it on to Jeffries. The other Angel, who has a black patch over one eye, hands back the camera.

I roll across the room until my wheels are almost touching Jeffries knees.

He looks down at the floor.

"So, Mr. Jeffries, what do you think?"

"Think?" he replies. "Think about what?"

"You know, whether I'm a phony benefits person or not."

"Oh, that," he laughs weakly. "Definitely not, Mr. Green. I can see you are what you claim to be, a genuine person with a disability. No question about that."

"And you were asked in for a cup of tea, a friendly cup of tea?"

He looks at the others and then back at me.

"Cup of tea," he says. "No question about that. Cup of tea."

"Friendly cup of tea," Paddy adds.

"Friendly cup of tea," Jeffries repeats. "That's exactly right."

Once again he begins to get up. I nod to Paddy, who doesn't intervene.

"One thing I would like to know before you leave, Mr. Jeffries."

"Of course," he says.

"Why me?"

"We had a call from someone who reported that you weren't actually disabled. That you were faking it."

"Faking it? I wish to hell I was! So who called you."

"I'm afraid I have no idea, Mr. Green."

"Wait. You do all this on the word of an anonymous caller?"

"That's how it works. If people had to give us their name, we'd not have many reports of fraud. I'm sure you can see that."

What I can see, is that someone wants to do me over.

"You OK now, Greenie," Paddy asks after Jeffries and the two bikers have left.

"Yeah, I'm good. Sort of anyway. What's worrying is who dropped the dime on me."

Paddy shrugs.

"For a bloke who's not been around here long, you seem to be pissing off a lot of people. That's for sure."

He's got that right.

Playing Offence

"He said that he had made some initial inquiries after I saw him on Tuesday," Sylvia says. "Even said he'd make further inquiries, but given how he reacted to Bob's story, I don't think that's going to happen this side of ever."

"Yeah. He said Piper was very well respected, a part-time magistrate even, that Motes was, in his words, 'a feckless nutter' and old Horse-Face Yallop had been with Social Services for twenty years and had been throughly checked out by the police so he could work with vulnerable people."

"Horse-Face!" Brendan hoots, "I guess he was checked to make certain he could make us more bloody vulnerable an' all."

"You know, do you," says Hedgy, "that the Gaines lads are the sons of those arseholes we helped put in prison? Surely even DC Richards could see they might want to do us harm."

"Never got to them," Sylvia replies. "Once he'd written off Yallop, Motes and Piper, that was more or less it for our suspicions and the story Delia told Bob. One positive thing though. They were looking more closely at what happened to Martin. Seemed to believe that might not have been an accident."

"Well," Ronald says, "that's something. Not much, but a start maybe."

We are all gathered again, this time at Hedgy's studio.

232

Outside the river windows light snow is falling, dusting with a tentative softness the half-submerged old tires and other floating junk. Inside, two big electric fan heaters hanging high up on the walls on either side of the room are roaring. They're making lots of noise but not much progress against the cold. The main thing they're doing is making the wheelchair tower sway back and forth and spinning around the dismembered motorcycle and impaled dummies.

As we came in I noticed Manpig is now wearing shades and there's a cigarette in a long white holder stuck in his mouth. Hedgy is dressed down in sequinned overalls, a frilly shirt and a straight, mid length auburn wig.

"You really think Delia Castle was murdered?" he asks.

"Don't know for sure, but if I had to put my money on it, I'd say yes. She wanted them to stop with the 'accidents' and they wouldn't. Logical next step, get rid of her before she could blab. After all, once you've bumped off five civilians, what's one more in the dumpster."

"Or another two," Ronald adds.

"You going to tell them about that snooper from the Social, Greenie?"

"Oh yeah, almost forgot. Happened right before we came down. Someone set this guy onto me from the benefits people. Said it was an anonymous call or something. No prizes for guessing who made the call. So, I figure enough already with this waiting-for-them bullshit. How about we start to play some offence, some serious offence?"

"Play what?" asks Hedgy.

"Football expression. I mean American football, not your limp-armed, limp-wrist, kick-the-ball-around crap."

"Bleeding Yank," Morris laughs.

"Offence, Greenie?"

"Yeah, Paddy. Let's take it to the bastards. Do it to them, before …".

"They do it to us," Ronald finishes.

"Accidents?" says Sylvia.

"Maybe."

"Oyi!" Hedgy shouts out, holding up a red-fingernailed-hand stop sign. "Wait just a bleeding minute. If I understand you correctly, you're suggesting we set about getting shot of all five of them? Well, I will tell you right now, even if they are killers, I for one will have nothing to with that kind of thing, Bob. No way."

"You can be such a prissy old toad, Vernon," Sylvia says.

Vernon? Whoa! No wonder he wanted to lose his first name.

"At least I've got style, lots of style, something you will never have."

I expect Brendan to jump in and break it up. He doesn't. Surprised by this, Hedgy and Sylvia lapse into a steaming silence.

"Not what I had in mind at all, Hedgy. Think I'm some kind of gangster or something? Give me a break here."

Paddy smiles broadly and finger-guns me.

"No, what I had in mind was to draw them out into the open. Get them to do something that exposes them for who they are and what they've done to your friends."

"Yeah. Set an ambush, like we did for the Taliban. Turned the tables on those rag-head bastards. Even put out some of our own IEDs to fuck them over."

"Besides the fact that we happen to be in Norfolk and not Afghanistan, what exactly are you suggesting?" Sylvia asks.

"One step at a time. First thing, we need some reliable intel. Over there we had drones and on-the-ground sources to sniff out what was going on. Here we got no eyes on the bad guys. Until we do we've got no hope of launching an effective counteroffensive."

"Same question, Ronald," Sylvia says.

Brendan suddenly explodes, squirms, slams backwards and gibber-spits something I can't catch. By their expressions, even Henry's, I'm not alone.

"Play that one more time, Brendan," I say.

"Easy," he says finally, grinning and throwing his arms all over the place. "Yallop's computer is an open book. I'll start there. If he's in contact with Piper and the others I'll be able to open up their computers too. Give me three or four days, and let's see what I can find."

3 or 4 Days Later

"**B**rendan, you found this stuff on all the computers?" Hedgy asks, dropping a thick yellow folder full of documents next to three or four other different colored folders stacked on an old pingpong table he's set up by the river window of his studio.

Hedgy rifles through another of the folders and pulls out some printed pages.

"On all the computers, but Motes', Brendan replies, "who, as far as I can tell, doesn't have a computer. Found loads of this stuff, but I'm not sure just yet exactly what it means."

"It means you've turned over a big slimy rock, Brendan. Dear God!"

"Want to share?" I say.

Hedgy looks up from the papers he's holding as if he's just seen me for the first time. His face is pursed and grey under the orangish pancake. Not a flattering combination of colors.

"Pardon?"

"Speak to us about the unspeakable, Hedgy."

He favors me with the evil eye, in this case two evil eyes, boiled-egg bulging under newly-plucked eyebrows.

"Come on man, lighten up will yah."

"This is no 'lighten-up', laughing matter, Bob. Not at all. What we've got, out there in lovely Hingham, Norfolk," he says, thrusting a fist full of papers at each of us in turn, "is a load of fucking Nazis."

"Oh, really!" Sylvia barks out so sharply that Hedgy flinches as if in pain. "So overly dramatic, Hedgy. Like always."

I wait for his usual quick-fire bitchy retort. It never comes. Instead, Hedgy slumps sideways in his chair and puts his face in his hands. With his head bowed, I see that today he's wearing an elaborately embroidered white yarmulke.

"Hedge?" Brendan says softly. "You OK? Hedgy?"

He tries to pat Hedgy on the back, but his comforting arm sails out in a long jerky arc, misses his shoulder and with Tom-and-Jerry inevitability smacks Hedgy up the side of his head, knocking the yarmulke flying. We all watch as it Frisbee-floats across the room, before coming to rest next to the remains of the executed wheelchair.

Paddy goes over picks it up and gives it back to Hedgy, who, staring down at the floor, turns it round and round in his hands.

"It didn't happen at all. Nope, not at all. A Jewish conspiracy, an international Jewish conspiracy it was. Six million? What six million? Gas chambers? What gas chambers? Photos? Oh, so easy to fake. Of course they are. On and on. It was the Americans, the Brits and the Russians who were the real war criminals, not the Nazis. Nuremberg was about winners punishing losers. Irving, Zundel, Bradley Smith and all the rest of the bastards. He's got them all, speeches, articles, the whole bloody lot. Wouldn't be surprised if he has a room in his house filled with Nazi memorabilia."

"Wait a minute, man," I say. "Slow down. Who are you talking about?"

"I'm talking about Maurice Piper. I'm talking about Yallop and Gaines and for all I know Motes as well. All caught up in the crooked-armed web."

"Nasty crap," I say. "Really nasty, but so what if Piper and his friends are fans of Adolf and Co? What does that have to do with us?"

Now they've got me going with the 'us' shit!

Hedgy smiles mirthlessly and shakes his head.

"So, what was it, Bob, before you changed it or your parents changed it? Greenberg? Greenwald? No, maybe Greenblatt?"

"So I'm a Jew, Hedgy. So what? Vernon Hedgy? What kind of kosher or even non-kosher Yid calls himself Vernon Hedgy?"

"The kind that, God knows how, survived Bergen-Belsen as a baby, was liberated by the British Army and after being passed from one displaced persons reception centre to another, was finally adopted by Mary Louise and Staff Sergeant Vernon Hedgy, the man who first found me in the camp."

Sylvia gasps.

"Hey, man," I manage, "I didn't know."

He reaches over and pats my hand.

"No way you or any of you could have known. Only Sarah knew. Only my lovely Sarah."

"Oh, Hedgy," Brendan says. "So sorry, mate."

"Parents?" I ask.

"How could I know? I was only a baby. My father said I was being hidden by a dying young girl in a building which was used by guards as a brothel. Probably my mother."

He rolls up the sleeve of his sweater and pushes his left arm across the table. A line of six faded blue numbers decorate his forearm.

"I was too young to be tattooed by the Nazis, so had this done myself so I would never forget. Yeah. So I would never forget."

It's strange how you don't notice that you're seeing a person in two dimensions until something happens and suddenly they're transformed into a fully three-dimensional being, just like you.

After a couple of minutes, Hedgy breaks the tense silence.

"Have any of you heard of Pastor Martin Niemöller? No. Well he wrote a famous poem about what happened in Germany. It goes,

First they came for the Communists

and I didn't speak out because I wasn't a Communist.

Then they came for the Socialists, and I did not speak out -

Because I was not a Socialist.

Then they came for the Trade Unionists, and I did not speak out -

Because I was not a Trade Unionist.

239

Then they came for the Jews, and I did not speak out -
Because I was not a Jew.

Then they came for me - and there was no one left
to speak for me.

"One group he didn't mention. Anybody?"

No one speaks.

"Incurables," Hedgy says. "Useless eaters. Lives
unworthy of life. Yes indeed, disabled people. We were
the first they came for, the very first to be scientifically
eliminated. Action T4. All was done in the name of
eugenic science, reducing both human misery and, of
course, the cost to the state, as well as improving the
physical and mental character of the German people.
Nice, huh?"

He picks up a folder and slams it down on the table.

"Friend Piper seems to be a particularly enthusiastic
follower of Action T4. Judging by the dates on the
documents, he'd embraced all that crap before you put a
spanner in his building plans. That incident just confirmed
his beliefs. Pushed him just that bit further. Like I said,
he's been forwarding the rubbish to the others. How
much they buy into it, I don't know."

"Obviously enough," I say, "so they think that a few
less disabled people here or there, isn't anything to worry
about."

The Smoking Gun

"Shall I be mother?" asks Morris, holding up the teapot.

"Not for me, thanks."

He pours cups for the others.

"Is what he's got on his computer illegal?" I ask.

"Don't think so," Hedgy replies. "It also doesn't prove he or his mates have murdered anyone. Would be bloody embarrassing though, if the news got out. Can't imagine many people wanting to hire a Nazi-loving architect. Gauleiter Yallop would most likely get the sack as well. The Brothers Gaines? Yeah, the Brothers Gaines. Well, I would guess being labeled as Nazis probably wouldn't sully their reputation any more than it already is, what with their parents in the nick for abusing crips."

"With the kinda friends they have, being a Nazi would most likely enhance their reputations," Ronald says.

"That's it then," I say. "We've got them by the short and curlies. Just need to leak this stuff to the press and they're screwed."

"I don't think so," Sylvia says. "Absolutely not. These people aren't simply fascists, they're fascist murderers. Shaming them, putting them out of business isn't enough, at least for me it isn't. I want them in prison. I want them in prison for a long, long time."

Hedgy and Brendan nod their agreement.

"Did you find anything in all that," I say pointing at the

folders, "that we can hang them with?"

"To be honest, I didn't really expect to find anything incriminating, at least directly incriminating. Didn't think they'd be sending each other emails saying, 'Let's arrange an accident for whoever' ".

"No smoking gun then, Brendan?"

"I wouldn't say that, Bob. No, wouldn't entirely say that."

He's doing a Cheshire Cat. Either that or he's got heartburn. Hard to tell, what with Brendan's curious, random gurning.

"Stop messing about," Sylvia tells him. "Come on, Brendan, spit it out. Please."

Where did I get the notion that blind people were especially sensitive?

"We've got emails, but most of those are his usual 'FYI' with links to neo-Nazi websites. But there is something curious going on if you look more closely."

"Can I have a butchers?" asks Hedgy.

"Green folder," Brendan says to Morris.

It's the thinnest one on the table. Morris picks it up, takes out maybe ten printed sheets and hands them to Hedgy, who studies them carefully.

"You'll see," says Brendan, "that he regularly sends out e-mails once a week, and they are sent to a long list of addresses, including Yallop's, the brothers Gaines and towards the end of the list to Delia Castle as well."

"So what," I say. "You've told us that already."

I gesture to Hedgy, who hands me the folder. I flip

through the sheets. Nothing but forwarded messages against lists of BCC email addresses.

"Do you see something I'm missing?" I ask Hedgy?

He shakes his head.

A bigger Cheshire Cat smile. If Brendan doesn't stop with this he's going to disappear, leaving us with only that shit-eating grin to deal with.

"OK. It's pretty elementary really," he says. "Maybe you just need the time to study the addresses more closely. If you did, you would see that every so often, five times to be exact, the weekly email goes out and doesn't include Yallop, the brothers or Delia. My best guess that's a prearranged message calling them to a prearranged meeting at a prearranged time and place. Very careful. Very cagy."

"Hold on now, Brendan, that's a pretty wild guess," Hedgy says.

"Perhaps. But if you check the dates when they are not included in the weekly postings, you'll see that the so-called accidents happened between two to three weeks afterwards. Each time, two to three weeks after."

"Interesting, Sherlock" I say, "but you'd have a hell of a job convincing the cops that there was anything incriminating in all this stuff. It's pure supposition. Doesn't stack up. I still think our best bet is what I said before, simply expose them in the press."

"Blue folder, Morris. Show them."

Morris takes out another bunch of papers and spreads them out. They're covered with printed charts. The first one I look at reads along the top of the chart entitled Call Log; Call Type, Caller Name, Contact Number, Call Start Time, Call Duration and Listen. Another chart is labeled SMS Log, another Emails. There are others as well.

"What's all this, Brendan?"

"Close as we're going to get to your smoking gun."

"Please," Sylvia says, "will somebody tell me what you're all looking at."

"We're looking at phone records, email records, GPS records and more. All from Yallop's private laptop, not the one he has at the Centre."

"So how'd you get to that?" I ask.

"Got the link through an email he forwarded to himself. Anyway, it appears that spyware's been put on all our phones. Yallop knew everything, who we called, who called us, all the text messages, emails, where we are at any time, he could even follow us, step by step, roll by roll".

"Wait," Sylvia interrupts. "How could they do something like that? Who could do something like that?"

"The how is easy," Brendan tells her. "You can buy the software on the internet. You only need to be able to put it on the target's phone and you've got their every move, their every communication. The who? Couldn't be anyone but old Horse Face. He must have slipped the apps on our phones when we were at the Centre. They're completely invisible too. No way to know we've been stitched up. Don't know how he got the others, but I remember he did ask once to see my new phone. Told me he wanted to buy one, so would I mind if he had a play with it."

"Yeah. I hear you. I just remembered when I first ran into Martin. He had dropped his phone in the bushes. Yallop appeared, got the phone for him and said he'd clean it up."

"He did that for sure," Brendan says. "Funny thing is he didn't send this information to the others. Only found it on his computer."

"Could be," I say, "that he phoned them with the info. Maybe figured it would be more secure that way."

"Oh my God!" Hedgy shouts out. "Oh my God. I'm still using Sarah's iPhone. It was better than the old thing I had, so I thought ...bloody hell!"

He jumps up and rushes over to a desk near the wheelchair tower. A few seconds later he comes back holding an iPhone at arms length, staring at it as if it was about to blow up in his hand.

"What the hell," he says, frantically pushing at keys, "How do we get rid of this stuff?"

"Hold on, I wouldn't do that right now, man."

"Why not, Bob?" Hedgy says, pausing, finger hovering uncertainly over the phone. "I don't want them following me, knowing what I'm doing."

"Because," Brendan interrupts, "they'll know we're on to them. Right, Bob?"

"Too true that."

"Let's just go to the police," Sylvia says anxiously. "Surely we've got enough here that even they can't ignore what it is."

"From what I've seen first hand," I say, "that police station leaks information like sweat from a longshoreman's armpit."

"Leaving aside that colourful simile," Hedgy replies, "Piper is a magistrate. You know how these things work. He's bound to hear about it when the police apply for a search warrant."

"Oh, please, Vernon. You are being rather paranoid, don't you think?"

Ignoring her, Brendan continues. "If they did find out we know what's going on they'll wipe their hard drives, ditch their phones, leaving us with nothing but piles of interesting but essentially legally useless paper."

"Because," I grab at the tail of his logic, "as we have already tried to put them in the frame with the cops, any two-bit lawyer will claim that we wanted…".

"To fit them up," Brendan finishes.

"As long as they don't know we know," I say, feeling the instincts from my old life flowing back strong and certain, "we can use this to mess them up so bad they'll be up to their necks in shit before they can smell it."

"Whatever that means, Amen!" Brendan gurgles, arms akimbo, as he rocks violently, crashing backwards in delight.

Gas Hill

It's 7:00 in the evening. It's freezing. The sidewalks are shining white with ice. An enormous yellow moon sits on the horizon. I'm rolling along the moonlit sidewalks, on my way to meet Brendan for a drink at the Butcher's Arms near Gas Hill. At least that's what Piper and friends will have picked up from our messages. It's our third attempt to lure them out. Given that it's now more than two weeks since the others failed to appear on Piper's email list, my tingling gut tells me that this time they've taken the bait and we're good to go.

"It's far too risky," Sylvia cautioned when I proposed doing this.

"Especially anywhere near to Gas Hill," Hedgy chipped in. "Not only is it like a hundred metres long with a twenty percent gradient but at the bottom it crosses Riverside Road. That's if you ever made it that far, which I very much doubt. Even if our cameras get it all, that won't do you much good if you end up as so much human roadkill."

"That's just the point, Hedgy. Gas Hill. It's the big draw. What place could be better for a waiting-to-happen accident? Those schmucks won't be able to resist it. Two guys in wheelchairs after a couple of drinks roll too close to the edge and down they go. You still up for it, Brendan? Yeah? Good. My guess is they'll make their move when we come out of the pub. Didn't we say that the two of us were going to roll back to my place where we'd meet up with Henry and the van? Even gave them the time we'd be leaving the pub."

Ronald was all for it, but thought we hadn't done it correctly, as his obsessive military preparations were being ignored.

"You've got responsibilities, Greenie," Molly said when she learned of the plan. "That child needs a parent, preferably one who's not dead or, you know."

"Crippled? Disabled?"

"OK, all of that. You know, Mr. Smartass, it could be a lot worse."

"Heard that refrain a few times. But listen, Molly, I'm good about this. Really. And Paddy's got my back."

"There's Henry and Morris as well," Paddy said. "They're a couple of handy blokes. I could always give Ralphie a bell."

I turned down that offer. Too many pieces moving around the board.

I've turned the corner of Telegraph Lane and am wheeling up St Leonard's Road towards the pub. I should have come from the other direction, but for some stupid reason, nerves maybe, turned too early and wound up going down Quebec Road. Once I did that the steep slope made it too difficult to stop and go back. So, I'd let myself roll down to Telegraph Lane and then cut back to St Leonard's Road. I start to push past Gas Hill, which is up about twenty feet on my left. Fifty yards away I make out the lighted pub sign. Paddy and the others should be waiting by now. The sidewalk is too narrow here, so I'm in the road. Now I don't feel so cocky. If they came for me in a car, there would be nowhere to go. Keep rolling. Come on, man, keep rolling! I push with more urgency. I'm not helped by the upslope. The chair has now begun to lose traction on the ice and is wobbling from side to side, as well as slipping backwards. I try to bring it straight by grabbing harder on the push rims. That only makes it swing more violently sideways. I feel like I am about to tip over. I sit up straight and let go of the rims, hoping the chair will right itself. Almost. Yes. Oh no! I've now turned all the away around. The chair is slowly picking up speed and heading back down the road away from the pub. I'll have to hold on tight and ride it out until I get to somewhere flat. Wow! The chair stops so suddenly that, but for the seatbelt, I'd have been thrown out onto the road.

"Good evening, Mr. Green," a voice behind me whispers. "Having a spot of bother, are we?"

This is not good.

"Were you trying to get to that pub? Of course you were. Let me give you a hand then."

I turn around. He's dressed all in black and wearing a dark watch cap. I can't make out the face, but the voice is not Yallop's. So, either one of the Gaines Brothers or Piper. Paddy and Co will be looking out for me coming from the other direction, and since we all figured they'd make their move later they will not be on high alert. Roland was right. Molly was right. Sylvia was right. I was dead wrong, soon to be just dead.

He's thrown a robe over me, pulled it tight, pinning my arms, swung the chair around and is pushing me up towards the pub and towards Gas Hill.

"Pad..!"

My yell is cut off by a gloved hand and a few seconds later a cloth gag.

"Now, Mr. Green, no need to cause a disturbance."

Another man appears from a driveway on the left. He doesn't say anything, but is helping to propel the chair, while the first man keeps a firm hand over my gagged mouth. We stop. The road down Gas Hill falls away in sharp dogleg to the right.

"Let's just take you a little further so you can enjoy the view before you go."

They push me down past the curve in the road, until I can see the full length of Gas Hill falling away steeply to where it crosses a main road a very long way down. The moon reflects off the black icy surface of the ski jump below me. It is hemmed in on one side by flint walls and a screen of bushes and on the other side by brick walls with houses behind them. Can I survive this? If I wasn't strapped in around the legs and waist I could throw myself clear, but I am trussed up like a damn convict.

"Not content with being a bunch of useless eaters and a costly social embarrassment, you people also think you've the right to interfere in what doesn't concern you. You especially, Mr. Green. If not for sticking your nose in where it didn't belong, we wouldn't be here and Delia Castle would still be alive. You have, I don't know, maybe ten seconds to mull that over on your way down. And just in case you're thinking that you might escape with only bruises or a few broken bones, I want you to look ten yards down on the right. See that driveway? See the headlights? Our colleagues are waiting in case you're in need of some assistance. So, this time I think we won't be having to wait on the bus or depend on a driver with too-quick reflexes. Well, goodbye then, Mr. Green."

The gag is yanked away. The rope comes off, hitting me in the face. The chair shudders and begins to move.

"Paddy! Paddy!"

I'm rolling. I'm rolling! Gathering speed. Wait. I'm not rolling. No. I'm sliding across the road towards the sidewalk on the right. I look down. Paddy's grinning face stares up at me. He's laying on the road, his arms wrapped around the frame of my wheelchair. It's a good thing he's wearing his leather gear because he's being dragged along. We skid and then bounce hard over the curb. The chair tips violently. Paddy manages to stop me going all the way over.

"Jesus H!"

"No need for blasphemy, Greenie. I always had your back."

Behind us I hear Brendan's loud garble of alarm. I hear Morris and Henry shouting. A body flies past, going down the icy hill. Another follows a second or two later. The first bounces hard once, twice and a third time before going into a sliding roll and stopping spread-eagled about half way down. The other tumbles more elegantly end over end, as if taking part in a gymnastic event, but comes to a less than elegant finish by going off the road and slamming headfirst into the flint wall.

For a few moments the only sound is of labored

breathing coming from Brendan and his gang at the top of Gas Hill. Then a motor roars, headlights flare and a car fishtales at speed out of the drive, slamming into the body on the road before continuing down the hill, the driver fighting to control it on the ice. He's not doing too well. Unable to stop at the intersection at the bottom of the hill, the car slides broadside straight across the road, mounts the curb and crashes into the low wall bordering the river. Two seconds later the noise of metal crunch and broken-glass tinkle reach us at the top of Gas Hill.

Love Hurts

When she walked into the restaurant, my first thought was that Gwen looked older than I remembered. Maybe it was because as she stood at the entrance looking around she appeared unsure, off balance, not connected. Maybe it was because in a black dress and silver necklace she was out of her usual skin. Now, sitting across the table I realize she's only radiating a different, a softer beauty than the hardscrabble one that had captured me so disturbingly at her place in the country.

Perhaps I too seem off balance and out of place or even younger than she remembered. She smiles warmly, reaches over and takes my hand.

"Not to worry, Bob, they'll think your mum's taking you out for a slap-up meal. Either that or I've got myself a lovely toy boy, a lovely disabled toy boy."

"Jesus, Gwen! Come on, I thought we got all that out of the way. Anyhow, who the hell cares what people think? Do you care?"

See glances at the other tables.

"No, not much. By the way, Paddy told me about what happened with those awful people. I'm sure that's a big relief for you. He also told me why you weren't mentioned in the papers or on the telly. So, Mr. Necessarily Modest, someone has to congratulate you."

She stands up, comes over and gives me a kiss on the top of my head.

Not good.

"Thanks, Gwen. I was just one of the team. No big deal."

"Well, I think it was a big deal, you putting yourself out there like you did. Stupid big deal, but still a big deal. You want to argue the toss with me on that?"

"Not really. I'd also like to get away from all that tonight. I've had a it up to here the last few days."

I had too. The police had been really furious. They said Brendan and his friends had been reckless and gone well outside the law and should have come to them with the evidence. When it was pointed out that they'd done precisely that, the cops quietly backed off. Over Sylvia's objections, the press never got that part of the story. They also never got wind of my involvement. Neither did the cops. Paddy wheeled me home straight away before the law arrived. We were never there. The story for both the cops and the press was that, besides being full, straight-armed Nazi sympathizers and responsible for killing five disabled people, and possibly Delia Castle as well, Yallop and Piper had tried to finish off Brendan by sending him on a one-way ride down Gas Hill. He was rescued by his two personal assistants. No one could tell it any other way. We wiped the cameras. Yallop was killed outright after being run over as he lay in the road. Maurice Piper had been so badly injured he had to be taken by helicopter to a hospital near Cambridge. He'd broken his neck and was in a coma, although it was thought he would come around.

"Bloody Nora!" Brendan had exclaimed. "Now the son of a

bitch is going to be one of us. What the hell is that all about?"

"Just desserts?" I'd ventured.

"No way," Brendan said. "Unless you see being disabled as some kind of punishment. Is that what you think, Bob?"

"Yeah, well, OK, ah, not really," I fumbled, although I did see it like that.

"Not to worry," Hedgy said. "You won't have to deal with the bugger, Brendan. They're going to put him away for a very long time."

"Yeah," I laughed, "then the mother can campaign for better access in the joint."

At that, Brendan nearly slam-laughed himself out of his wheelchair.

For me one of the best things to come out of that mess was, from what Piper had said, it was them, not the Russians, who engineered my run in with the Number 16 bus. I am home free or, if not exactly home, at least Anna and I are out from under. For right now anyway.

"Hey, Gwen, can we talk about something else, please?"

"OK, let's talk about something else. If it's not too sensitive, one thing I did wonder about was whether your father ever remarried?"

"Nope, he never did. I was brought up by two men, my father and my Uncle Sol, who thinking back, I now reckon was probably gay. And I know where you're going with this. Been taken there before. And no, I am not attracted to you because I never had a mother. OK?"

Luckily, a more extended, self-serving and ultimately pathetic tirade is forestalled by the appearance at the table of our waitress.

"Are you ready to order, please?" she asks.

I detect an Eastern European accent. Russian? Perhaps. I look at her more carefully.

A very tiny, pretty young woman with large green eyes and jet black hair pulled back in a ponytail. One thin arm is fully covered in a bright, multicolored swirling tattoo of flowers, leaves and vines. On the back of her left hand is a smiling cat wearing a bow tie. Not my idea of an assassin, but aren't they the ones you have to watch out for? No. Surely not. Just a young girl. What the hell am I thinking here? All that crazy shit that happened was Norwich-grown, not imported. Still, what if...? Before I can dig myself a deeper trench of paranoia, Gwen intervenes.

"May I ask you something, dear?" she asks. "Who did your arm?"

"Oh, that," the girl replies, twisting the arm in front of her to admire it. "From Red Molly. Works at studio on Magdalen Street. Very good, she is. No?"

"Yes indeed," Gwen laughs. "She's my daughter. Thought I recognised her work."

"Oh, must be very proud of your daughter," the waitress says. "Red Molly is best, absolutely best."

Gwen glows with maternal pride.

"Thank you."

The girl smiles at Gwen and then sneaks a measuring look at me. Probably trying to figure out our relationship. If she manages to do that, maybe she'd clue me in.

After she takes our order and goes off, Gwen, apparently deciding that she'd be safer avoiding the Oedipal schtick, asks, "What about your wife, Bob?"

"Ex."

"OK, your ex wife. You never told me much about her. A painful subject?"

"No, not really. Gwen, tonight I'd rather talk about you and me. What's happened, has happened. Nothing you can do about it."

"Maybe not. But you can learn, Bob. At least I hope you can. I know I have. Learned a lot."

"And so, what have you learned?"

"Well, for starters, I've learned there is no 'you and me'. There's you and then there's me.' Like I told you before, I'm not in the market for making those kind of 'you and me as one' compromises."

"Pretty cynical, don't you think?"

"I'd say pretty realistic, Bob."

"And that's what you've learned? Learned from your fling with that Jewish guy?"

"Oh no, Bob, not from that, although I should have. No, I learned from a number of other, too many other 'you and me' things. It took me too long to come around to figuring out what did and didn't work for me. Not that I haven't enjoyed being with other people - men and women. Bob? Oh dear, now I've shocked you."

"I'll get over it, Gwen."

"Don't, Bob. Don't get over it. Get past it. A big difference."

I think I'm about to be hung out to dry.

"As I was saying, I've had a number of what you might call 'significant relationships' and each has, in the end, come to grief because, well, maybe because of me, maybe the other person, but what I could never deal with was being possessed by someone, or being possessed by someone's idea about who they want me to be."

"And here is stupid me thinking we were going to have a nice romantic meal together."

"Oh, Bob, please. I hope we are going to have a nice romantic meal. Nothing I'd like more. Can't we have that with eyes open, no smoke and mirrors? I like you very much. You're very good company."

"That's it?"

"Bob, Bob, please don't try to misunderstand me. We enjoy being with each other, don't we? Yes? OK, so let's get on and enjoy our romantic evening together."

"I am almost afraid to ask, Gwen, but what about love? Can romance live without it. Where does love fit into your relationship equation?"

"Love? God knows, Bob. If I could… Wait a minute, are you making a declaration?"

"You know," I laugh uncertainly, "I don't know what I'm doing. My life has been so screwed up the last year or so, what with having to abandon the only life I've ever known, go on the run with my daughter, being hunted, living in a strange country and stranger city, finding that I'm poor for the first time in my life, then finding myself stuck in this wheelchair, I haven't had any time to think about love, finding it, knowing when I'm … Damn it! I don't know what I am even trying to say here. Listen, Gwen, excuse me for a couple of minutes, will you?"

I spin the chair around and head for the john. I don't want her to watch me lose it completely, which I am just about to do. Yanking open the door to the disabled restroom, I propel myself inside and slam the door behind me.

I take two, three, four very deep breaths, run the faucet until the sink is full of cold water, slowly lower my face into it.

The worst part is that I think I may be in love or falling in love with this impossibly realistic grandmother.

Have You Met Miss Jones?

"**Y**es, this is Mr. Green speaking."

"First let me say that there is no need to be worried."

That's the last thing I want to hear from the head teacher at Anna's school. This kind of call is every parents' nightmare. Fear is stomping all over me. Everything is outline clear but makes no sense at all. I have to focus. Anna. Anna. Nothing else matters. Anna.

"Has something happened? Is Anna all right?"

"She's fine, Mr. Green. Just fine."

I hear my pulse racing. I exhale and only then realize I've been holding my breath.

"So why are you calling?"

"Was a Miss Jones supposed to collect Anna early from school today?"

Another wallop of terror hits me. I've relaxed too damn soon. They're still out there. They're after my little girl.

"No way. Absolutely not. Where is she now?"

"She's here in my office, Mr. Green, along with Harley and his mother."

"Thank God! Jesus! Tell me what happened. Please."

Calm, Bobby. Calm down. You won't do Anna any good if you spin your wheels. Focus. Focus.

"I think it would be better if you came here, Mr. Green. This is something I'd prefer not to discuss over the phone or in front of your daughter." Her voice drops to a whisper. "Also, I will now have to call the police. Standard procedure. I'm sure you understand."

I see another visit from DS Richards coming down.

"Of course, you do. Police. Right, I'm on my way. Be there is soon as I can. Could I talk to Anna, please?"

"I haven't said anything. No point upsetting her."

"I appreciate that. I'll just have a word, if that's all right."

I hear her calling to Anna.

"Daddy?"

"Hi darling. You OK?"

"I'm fine, Daddy. Am I in trouble for something bad I did?"

" 'Course not, sweetheart. Mrs. Padmore was just telling me what a good girl you've been. In fact, she wants me to come over there right now so she can tell me in person more about how good you've been. I'll see you in a few minutes. OK?"

"OK, Daddy. See you."

Lucky for me Paddy is in his shed at the back with one of his friends dismantling or maybe mantling a Harley. It's hard to tell.

"Real quiet for all these months, and then out of nowhere you're hit by a shit storm, Greenie."

"Sure seems that way. Ever since I met up with Legless Ben, it's all been going South."

Paddy helps me into the van, and five minutes later we're in front of the school yard. Parents are filing out, kids in hand. They are all walking at an angle into the wind and driving rain. As we pull up, Molly and the two children come running out with Mrs. Padmore, a stout, reassuringly no-nonsense woman in her late fifties. She's sheltering under a black, no-nonsense umbrella.

"I think it would be better if Mr. and Mrs. Driscoll take the children home, Mr. Green," Mrs. Padmore says.

"I'll drop them and come back and collect you," says Paddy. "You don't want to be pushing yourself home in this weather."

They all pile into the van and drive off. Sharing her umbrella, I roll with Mrs Padmore into the school.

Worn linoleum corridors, institutional green doors and children's drawings on the walls. Down at the end of the hallway, an overalled man is cleaning the floor, swinging the mop back and forth in slow, broad strokes. She leads me into her office. The walls are lined with metal filing cabinets and piles of paper are on her desk, on the tops of the cabinets, on the floor. The room smells of boiled tea and damp.

"Can I get you a cup of tea, Mr. Green."

"No thanks. I'm fine. I'd really like to know what happened today."

"Tell you what, Mr. Green. If you wait right here for a few minutes I'll fetch Miss Garvey, Anna's teacher, who first spoke to the lady and hopefully the police will be here by the time I return."

Ten minutes later Mrs. Padmore comes back with a hefty young woman wearing glasses and severely unhappy hair. She's clutching a handkerchief and her eyes are red-rimmed. Before she can be introduced,

262

two uniformed cops, a man and a woman, appear at the office door.

"Mrs. Padmore?" asks the woman, who is wearing sergeant stripes.

They introduce themselves. I've got fears about Anna filling my mind and there is no room left for their names to take up residence. Maybe she is someone Rachel sent to find Anna. Better that than the other possibility.

Miss Garvey starts to sob. "I am so sorry," she says, her shoulders heaving up and down. "I almost let that woman take her. What was I thinking? Oh dear, what was I thinking?"

Mrs. Padmore puts her arm around the younger woman.

"It's OK, Gloria. Nothing happened. You did absolutely the right thing. Anna is just fine."

The two cops look on impassively.

"She said she was a family friend," sobs Gloria Garvey, "and that you asked if she could collect Anna before school finished because you had to catch an early afternoon train to London."

"What did this woman look like?" the female cop asks, pen poised above her notebook.

"Glasses and short, I think blond, hair. Sort of normal height. A normal looking person, to be perfectly honest."

"Clothing?" asks the other cop.

She squints as if trying to visualize the woman.

"Darkish suit. I think that's right. Very respectable looking. Normal really. Just normal, to be perfectly honest."

"Old? Young? White? Black?"

"Oh, no," she laughs uneasily. "I would remember if she'd been black."

"How old?"

"Hard to say. Maybe 30s. Sort of ...".

"Normal for someone in their 30s?" the male cop finishes her sentence.

Miss Garvey blushes.

"Anything not normal about her?" the woman asks, trying without success to keep the annoyance out of her voice. "Anything distinctive?"

"Not really. Can't think of anything, to be perfectly honest. Although, of course, she did have an American accent."

The two cops look at each other. 'Disbelief' does not do justice to their exchange.

"You sure it was American?" I ask.

"Oh yes," she replies. "Sounded just like you, Mr. Green. Well, almost anyway. To be perfectly honest, I don't have a very good ear for accents. Never did. It's hard to miss an American accent though, isn't it."

I reckon the Perfectly Honest Miss Garvey could miss a drunken gorilla tap dancing in an elevator.

"Please tell us exactly what happened, Miss Garvey," the sergeant says. "One step at a time."

The teacher recounts how the woman came to the door of the classroom, asked about picking up Anna, how she was about to call to her when she noticed the woman was looking around and although Anna was quite

264

close by she didn't seem to recognize her.

"That's when I got suspicious and remembered that visitors are supposed to check in at the office first, especially if they haven't collected a child before. So, I asked her if she had done that. She said she had and I asked for the permission slip. She looked in her handbag and said she must have lost it, but assured me it would be OK. She was very polite. Then I was on the point of calling to Anna, when Mrs. Padmore came by and told Miss Jones that she would have to phone Mr Green just to check that it was OK."

"Then," Mrs. Padmore continues, "she said she needed to fetch something from her car and would be right back. That's the last we saw of her."

"Any idea of who this Miss Jones might be," the male cop asks me.

"No. None at all. I don't know anyone named Jones, and I'm definitely not catching a train to London."

"Know anyone who might want to harm your daughter or you?" the sergeant asks.

"God no," I reply with a dismissive chuckle, hoping I sound convincing enough without overdoing it.

"OK," the sergeant says, giving me the once over.

After all these years of having to bump up against them, I never cease to be amazed how when you're the victim of a crime, cops want to put you in the frame. I guess it makes their job easier. After all, you're right there. The bad guys they've got to go out and find.

"We'll make a report," she says. "Miss Garvey, you

may have to come down to the station to complete a formal incident report. Depends on what CID say. As for you, Mrs. Padmore, I doubt she'll return to the school, but just in case please let all your staff know what happened and tell them to report anything suspicious, anyone unfamiliar hanging around. Mr. Green, I would advise you to keep a very close watch on your little girl. Very close. I want you to know we take this kind of thing extremely seriously. So, Mr. Green, when you get the child settled we will pay you a visit at home or if it is more convenient you could come down to Bethel Street. Let me know. Here's my number."

She hands me a business card. Sergeant M. Fisher.

"If in the meantime, call us straight away if you have any concerns, any concerns at all."

Concerns? These people don't know from concerns.

Never Underestimate

"**D**o you know anyone who would want to harm your daughter?" asks Sergeant Fisher.

I decided to go down to the Bethel Street Police Station rather than having more curious police eyes in the house. We're not in the same interview room, although it looks exactly the same.

Sergeant Fisher is maybe late 20s. Blue eyes and short, dark hair. Her face looks softer without the cap. Softer or not, she is all business.

"No. Like I told you at the school, we've never had any reason to be concerned."

"You've received no threats of any kind?"

"None."

She flips open a folder on the table in front of her. It seems familiar.

"I see here," she says, "that you told PC Gomes up at the hospital that you were pushed in front of a bus. Let's see. Last month. On the 25th of the month to be exact."

"I thought I straightened that one out with one of your detectives."

She turns a couple of more pages.

"Yes, that would be Detective Sergeant Richards? He says here that you did change your story, as you say. However, now with what has happened at the school, he has asked me to review your account of the incident at the crossing in order to confirm there is no connection between the two events. After all, Mr. Green, we are now talking about the safety of a small child."

"Sure thing. Really though, Sergeant, it was nothing more than an accident. Believe me, I would be the first to let you know if I thought there was the least connection. Anna's safety always comes first for me."

"Where is your daughter now, Mr. Green?"

"Oh, she's with my neighbor and Harley, her son."

"I see. Well, to make sure, we'll be putting a plainclothes woman constable in her school for a week or so. For all the children will know, she'll be a temporary classroom assistant."

"That's very thoughtful," I say.

There's a knock on the door, and it is followed into the room by Detective Sergeant Richards.

"Well, Mr. Green, here you are again. I'm glad you could get down to the station. Saves me a trip."

"Does it? I've been telling the other Sergeant here that my little girl is safe and sound. Nothing to worry about."

"Pleased to hear it. Really pleased. She's a lovely little girl. Anna?"

"That's right, Anna."

"I'm sure you will understand our concern, Mr. Green, especially after what happened.

"Yeah, the accident. I know."

"I'm afraid that's not all, Mr. Green. You seem to have become, I don't know how to put this, sort of a serial incident magnet, if you know what I mean."

Quite an unorthodox, off-the-playbook mouthful for a copper.

"Sorry, I don't follow."

I follow him all too easily.

"Smoke and fire, Mr. Green. Smoke and fire."

"OK, I'll bite."

"When someone's name keeps cropping up, as yours has, we are forced to at the very least try to see if we can join up the dots."

"Really, Sergeant, I'm not sure what you're trying to tell me."

"What he's saying," Sergeant Fisher adds, "is that it is unusual, unless of course you were one of our repeat offenders, which you're not, for someone's name to come up again and again linked to different incident reports."

"Thank you, Sergeant," says Richards, "would you mind? I'd like a private word with Mr. Green."

She gives him a questioning stare but picks up her file and walks out of the room without a word.

"Besides this unfortunate business with your daughter," Richards says. "I'm sure you've read the papers about what happened to your friends."

"Meaning Brendan and his carers. Of course."

"And that what we've found out is more or less what you and Miss Banning told me the other day."

"That's right. I'm glad that's been all cleared up."

"I'm to understand that you had nothing to do with the events that took place on Gas Hill?"

"Is there any reason to believe I did, Sergeant?"

"Not at this time, Mr. Green. However, it does seem curious that one day someone comes with an unlikely tale to tell and not long after it becomes a likely tale. That's to say nothing about one of the main characters in that tale being found dead and another critically injured."

"Well," I say, "first of all, that tale was not mine, but the late Mrs. Castle's. Secondly, I am pleased that it has all worked out. After all, Sergeant Richards, who wants a load of Nazis going around murdering disabled people? As a disabled Jewish person, not me. That's for damn sure."

So there's me then, Bob Green - a self-proclaimed disabled Yid - out of the closet of my 'it's only temporary' identity.

"I see. Well, thanks again for coming in. As I'm sure DS Fisher told you, we'll have a plainclothes officer at the school for about a week. You keep a close watch on that little girl, Mr. Green."

He puts out his hand. I take it and look him square in the eyes, wearing my most sincere expression. He may be a fat, bald cop in an English backwater, but I sense that it would be a big-time mistake to underestimate him.

Surfacing

As we pull up and park the van, I see a couple of Paddy's buddies outside sitting astride their Harleys. I can't be sure, but I think they're the same ones who rousted that jackoff from the government.

Once we're inside Molly and Paddy's place, one of the bikers asks Paddy, "Seen the EDP today, Boss?"

"No, can't say that I have, Ralphie. Why, something I should know about?

"Reckon so," Ralphie says, slapping the newspaper onto the kitchen table.

Still standing, Paddy leans straight-armed on the table and reads.

"Bloody hell!" He shouts out. "It ain't him. It ain't bloody him, not even close."

"Who him isn't it?" I ask, unable to find a more elegant choice of words.

Paddy hands me the newspaper.

Body of Missing Man Found in Quarry.

Underneath is a photo of a thin young guy in a suit. He's smiling.

'The body of Jerome Jeffries, an inspector with the Department of Work and Pensions, was discovered yesterday by two men who were out coarse fishing in a disused quarry near Holt. Jeffries, a married man with three small children, had not been seen for over two weeks. The police say...'.

"So then who the hell was that guy we saw?" I ask.

"Not Jeffries, that's for dead certain," Paddy says.

The handmade shoes! I should have known they didn't fit that picture. People always forget to change their shoes. A giveaway I missed completely. Me, with the practiced eye for it too. Schmuck!

"Why would anyone want to murder some poor bugger," asks Ralphie, "just to play stupid games with your mate here? Don't make no sense."

Obviously, Paddy didn't tell them about my Russian friends.

"Who's saying the bloke was topped?" Paddy asks.

"Come on, man," Ralphie insists. "They find a body in a quarry and we get some bloke on the doorstep using his name and giving grief to your mate Bob here. What else but murder?"

"You reckon we should maybe make a call?" asks the other biker, who wears the black eyepatch. "Anonymous like, 'course."

"I vote for keeping well clear of this one, Nelson," Paddy says. "Real clear."

"No way you gonna be able do that, Paddy," says Ralphie. "That dead bloke sure ain't coming back, but the other one, who, thinking back on it looked as if he might be a lot harder than he made out, he'll be back. Count on it."

"How you figure?" Nelson asks.

"Because," Ralphie explains, "he ain't going to all the bother to kill the real Jeffries, without doing whatever it

272

was he killed him for. Stands to reason."

"And that would be?"

"How the fuck should I know, Nelson. But whatever it is, I reckon Bob here is in the frame. Bob?"

"Beats the shit out of me," I shrug, trying to look more perplexed than concerned.

No doubt about it. The Russians, or at least someone they've hired, have found me. It's been a few days since the phony Jeffries paid a visit. That was a couple of days before the woman tried to lift Anna from her school. It wasn't Rachel then. Although maybe there is no connection between the two of them. Maybe she was working for Rachel and he is working for the Odessa mothers. Whoever they are, I've got to get us out of here. Where the hell can we go? How did they get so close? Too many questions. Only one answer. Time to run, Bobby.

"You want us to stick around for a bit, Paddy?" Nelson asks, planting his feet wide and squaring his shoulders as if the phony Jeffries was about to barrel through the door. "Won't be a cuppa we'll give him this time around. No sir, it won't."

Tough as these guys might be, they'll be no match for a couple of pros, even one pro.

"Yeah," adds Ralphie. "Soon as he spots this in the paper, that bloke's got to make a move. Stands to reason."

Nelson goes to the window and squints with his one good eye out into the woods across the road. Paddy looks at me. I shake my head.

"Thanks, boys. I reckon if he's seen this, he'll been long gone by now."

"How do you figure that?" Ralphie asks.

"OK, Ralphie. Right now let's say he's sitting in a cafe somewheres having a cuppa and reading this newspaper. What's he thinking? I'll tell you what. He's thinking that we're sitting here reading the same newspaper and then, just like Nelson here wanted to do, we're straight on to the Old Bill. Yeah? So, here is just about the last place he's gonna be visiting. Too hot. I tell you for sure, long gone he is. Stands to reason, don't it, Ralphie?"

"And if he ain't got the newspaper to be reading it?"

"Believe me," I say, "if he's who I think he is, he's reading that newspaper."

"And who you thinking it might be?" Ralphie asks.

"Well, let's just say I've got some very nasty folks who have been after me for a while, and I reckon now they've found me. Nasty as they are, they're also very careful, very professional. So they'd be keeping an eye on the newspapers, listening to radio, watching the TV news to make dead certain poor Mr. Jeffries hasn't surfaced. Since he has, I mean literally surfaced, that doesn't mean they won't come back, but I reckon not until things have cooled down some."

"You are a dark one, Bob," Ralphie says. "Sure as shit, you are. So, who are these 'folks', as you call them?"

"Probably better you don't know."

"You saying we can't take care of business here?" Nelson snarls, slamming his beefy fist into his beefy hand. "We sorted him out before, we'll sort the bugger again, don't you worry none about that."

"Appreciate it, man, really I do, but these people aren't your every-day, run-of-the-mill kind of thugs. That guy we saw is either a hitter or is scoping out the ground for a hitter. The best thing to do, the only sensible thing to do is avoid them, if you can. And that's exactly what I'm fixing to do. I'm going to take my little girl, get out of here and lay low for a while. No need for you guys to get mixed up in this any more than you have already."

"We can get us guns," Nelson says. "No worries about that, mate. We'll see you alright."

"It's OK, Nelson," says Paddy. "If we need you, I'll give you a bell. Right?"

Nelson seems doubtful and is about to say something when Ralphie starts towards the door.

"You sure on that, Boss?" he asks, turning back to Paddy. "You're talking guns here. We could hang if you want."

"It's OK, Ralphie. We'll be good. Like I said, he's sure to have done a runner. Not to worry now."

Ralphie pauses at the door.

"Oh yeah, I forgot," he says, reaching for something in his jacket pocket. "Didn't think this was any big deal at the time, but now, well, here."

He walks across the room and drops a small digital memory card into Paddy's outstretched hand.

"Nelson here nicked it from that bloke's camera. Never did care much for them snoopers."

"Nice one, Nelson," Paddy says.

"You got it then, Paddy. Come on Nelson, let's roll. Mind how you go, boys."

"And you mind the snow," Paddy calls after them.

A minute later, one bike roars and then the other joins in chorus. The noise rises, changes tone as they engage their engines and then fades, rising once more as they shift gear at the corner and then the sound slowly ebbs away.

Germans

It's a good thing Anna and I don't have a lot of carry. I managed to fit everything we need, in fact, everything we've got, into three medium-sized suitcases. More difficult was having to explain to Anna why we were once again on the move.

"It's just for a few weeks, Pumpkin," I lie. "We'll be back home before you know it."

"All the way back? Back with Mommy?"

"That too. Sure thing. But first we'll go back to Norwich and then not long after we'll be able to go see Mommy again. OK?"

She takes a deep, shuddering breath and, while trying as hard as she can to hold it back, begins noiselessly to weep rivulets of tears far too large for her face.

"I want to see Mommy," she sobs. "Please, Daddy, I miss her so so much. I not seen her for so so long now. Please, Daddy, please can we go all the way back home, the real back home? Pretty please!"

Now it's my turn to fight the tears. I love this small person so damn much it hurts. Sunk deep in my own worries, I often forget the gnawing uncertainty, the pain of separation from her mother and friends she must be feeling all the time. With me now stuck in this damn wheelchair, how much more uncertain and vulnerable does she feel?

"You alright, Anna?" Molly asks, turning around from the front seat of the van.

"Thank you," snuffles Anna.

We're on the road out to Gwen's place. It's two in the afternoon and getting dark. The sky's layered black with clouds and the snow has turned from fairyland flakes to fat plonking pellets. The windshield wipers are struggling as they judder against the onslaught. Paddy has to lean forward, his face almost touching the glass, to see the road ahead. How does anyone get used to this shit?

As soon as Nelson and Ralphie left the house, Paddy did a complete 180.

"We got to get the hell out of here, Greenie. I mean all of us. As soon as."

"I'm with you there. By the way, nice snow job with your friends. You almost had me convinced."

"Well, that's was what I thought that look you gave was telling me."

"What else? I've got no idea if that prick would be reading a newspaper or any of it. My best guess is if he had, then he would be coming around sooner than later. He'd know for sure I wouldn't go to the cops and blow my cover, but instead I'd pack up and get out of town."

Paddy called Molly to come back straight away from the tattoo parlor. Then he called one of his uncles in Ireland and asked if he could put Anna and me up for a little while.

"Paddy, you don't need to do that, man.'

"You got a better plan?"

"Not really. I'm still working out what to do. Whatever, Norwich sure as hell's not safe for us anymore."

278

"Shitty deal, especially now you've sorted out those Nazi scumbags good and proper."

"True enough. And that's a 'we' for the sorting out, man. I'll never forget your face grinning up at me, when I thought I was headed straight for the boneyard. A genuine, last minute goal-line tackle that was."

"Whatever. That was then, this is now. Let's go, Greenie."

By the time the kids came back from school with Molly, we were packed. Just in case someone had an eye on us, Anna and I got a cab to the railway station, walked and rolled in through the front doors, hung out for about half an hour and then went out a side exit, got in another cab and met Paddy, Molly and Harley a few blocks away.

A gust of wind throws a horizontal blast of heavy snow against the side of the van making it shudder to one side. The kids scream, delighted with their fear.

"Is your mother expecting us, Molly? Does she know why we're coming?"

"That's a yes and a no. Figured better to fill her in when we get there. I told her we were coming for a cup of tea. No need for her to be worrying."

"She doesn't strike me as a worrier."

"You'd be surprised," Molly says. "Our Gwen's like a bloody duck, all smooth gliding, no bother on the surface, while paddling like buggery underneath."

"Grandma is not a duck!" Harley protests loudly. "She's not. I'm going to tell."

"And she's got Germans behind her toilet," Anna adds.

"Germans? Behind the toilet?"

"Yes, Daddy. That's where they are. She said. Gwen did."

"Said we can't play there because of the Germans," Harley says. "They'll get us ill, they will. The Germans do that".

Megaliths in the Snow

The only up side of our having to escape from Norwich is that I'll get a chance to see Gwen once more before we move on. That's the only downside as well. Our nice romantic meal had not ended particularly nice or particularly romantic.

"You look unwell, Bob. What's the matter?"

I had returned from the bathroom, water dripping from my hair, still struggling with my wildly confusing emotions. It obviously showed.

"I'll be fine. Really. Another glass of wine would help. Yeah, that should do it."

She filled my glass, then put her hand on mine and gazed sadly across at me.

"I've been thinking, Bob. Given where you are at the moment, what you need at the moment and where I am and what I need, I don't think seeing each other is such a great idea for either of us. I can see you're hurting, that you want something from me that I can't give you. It's a shame, a real shame, but there it is. It would be too emotionally risky for both of us. Much, much too risky."

"Wait, Gwen, just wait, please. Look I'll be, I mean, we'll be OK. What I mean is that I'll be OK and you'll be OK and, you know, then everything will be OK. We just have to take it slow. Take it… Oh, shit, what am I saying? Who am I kidding? Right. You know something? Maybe you're right. No, not maybe. I am a disaster area, aren't I? So, there you are. One hundred percent, there you are."

After that there was a lot more to say, but whatever it was, neither of us could find it. We finished our dinner, she drove me home, gave me a motherly peck on the cheek and that was it. I felt terrible. When I had time to reflect, I felt relief and then terrible again for feeling relieved. Any romance is hard work and with all that was going on, especially the need to concentrate on shielding Anna and myself from all the heavy shit that had been coming down, a relationship with someone like Gwen, who I decided was way too grownup for me and was going to be way too tough for my too young, too stupidly innocent Californian heart.

We've turned off the main road and then a few minutes later off the secondary road onto the narrow dirt track leading to Gwen's. Except for the high hedges on either side, there is no way to see where the track is. The van hits something, slews and gently bumps side on up against a bank of snow. The kids gasp in unison, but no screaming. They are really frightened.

"It will be OK, children," says Molly, but the ever so slight hesitation in her voice betrays her.

"Mummy, are we stucked?"

"Daddy," Anna pipes up, "Can me and Harley make a snowman now?"

She's never seen snow before.

"Sit down, Harley. You too Anna," Paddy says, putting the van in reverse and slowly backing into the centre of the track. "Good thing the snow's still soft enough that we've got us some purchase on the gravel underneath."

He engages the clutch and after a slight juddering

we're off again, into what has become almost a total whiteout. Using the tops of the hedges as guides, Paddy drives on, until about ten minutes later we arrive and slide ever so gracefully into the yard between the house and the barn. I look out the window to find we are in the middle of a smooth white landscape surrounded by Gwen's tall, rust-red steel sculptures wearing powdery crowns, thrusting high out of the snow, looking more than ever like abandoned megaliths left by visitors from another world.

"Come on, Harley, Anna," Molly says. "Let's get our stuff and get in out of the cold."

"Where is Caro and Smith at?" Harley asks.

"Your gran has probably put them in the barn," Paddy explains. "They're tough old dogs, but she don't want 'em freezing to death now, does she?"

The two kids jump from the van, but instead of going inside they start throwing handfuls of snow at each other. They're so excited they can't even take the time to make snowballs.

Under my weight the wheelchair sinks firmly into the snow. I can't move. It takes the combined power of both Paddy and Molly to get me across the yard from the van, up the plywood ramp and into the house. Meanwhile, Harley and Anna, shrieking with the glee, are running and falling and throwing snow at each other and up in the air. For them snow is a magical gift. For me it's just another pain in the ass thing that shrinks my world. No fun at all.

"Mum, you home?" Molly calls out.

"We're in here," a woman's voice answers.

We carry on through the kitchen and into the living room, where we find Gwen. She's gagged and tied to a wooden chair with a mummy-like wrapping of green duct tape. Blood is caked on her forehead, one eye is badly bruised and it looks as if she is unconscious. A tall woman, wearing dark blue coveralls, black gloves and a full head, rubber Minnie Mouse mask with big sticking out ears and a Mickey-Mouse-Club grin, is standing by her side. She's cradling Gwen's 12 gauge, both barrels propping up Gwen's chin. Minnie has a pistol in her waistband. On the couch behind them sits Mickey Mouse, also in coveralls, gloves and the patent grin. I figure him for the fake Jeffries. He's holding a discreet Glock 9mm and pointing it not so discreetly in our direction.

The only good news are the masks. If they don't want to be identified, it's because they don't intend to waste all of us.

"Mr. Fishbaum," Minnie says, with a distinct, although I reckon a put-on, Southern drawl, "Mr. and Mrs. Driscoll, welcome. Please don't do whatever you are thinking of doing. Your mother did, and see what it got her. We'd hate to get more blood on the floor. You know, it's a real bitch getting stains out of wooden floorboards."

Out in the yard the kids' racket of delight continues.

Minnie and Mickey

"That should be good enough," Minnie says, as she tugs on the ropes Mickey has used to tie Molly and Paddy to each other back to back on the floor.

Curiously, Mickey has not said word one since we came in fifteen minutes ago. It's been totally a Minnie Mouse gig. He's the silent support act.

"Nothing to say? That's too bad. Then no goodbyes to Mr. Fishbaum, I'm afraid. And what do you have to say to your friends, Mr. Fishbaum? No goodbyes from you either, I expect. You sure? No apologies for getting them into such an awful mess?"

Unlikely. We've all been gagged with green duct tape.

We're gagged because Minnie told us they had a job to do and it was not up for discussion or argument or deals of any kind.

"In a way, you all, I mean Mr. and Mrs. Driscoll and the old lady and of course, the little kiddies too, are real lucky," Minnie had said after we'd been gift wrapped. "We've only got one contract and that's for Mr. Fishbaum here. You're also lucky that we're business people, not homicidal Manson crazies or the folks we figure are paying us for all this. They're a pretty darned crazy bunch. Wouldn't have hesitated to decorate the walls with all you nice folks. Kiddies too. No sir, they indeed would not hesitate. So lucky you. And here's the part I really enjoy. I'm sure you all will humor me, won't you? Thank you oh so much for that. We wanted you to know, all this here is not personal, it's strictly business. Don't you just love it? Well, sure enough I can see how maybe not."

That damn movie is playing me into my grave.

"The body, or rather the body parts, who, as our note will explain, did not belong to Robert Green but to an American named Robert Fishbaum, who is, I mean was, nothing but a smalltime hood who crossed some badass folk back in Los Angeles. So, with no mass murder to rile folks, no dead kiddies either, who's going be to real upset about one more dead hood, especially a dead American hood?"

Body parts! Oy gevalt! I pull as hard as I can but the ropes hold me tight to the wheelchair. I try to shout. Nothing but a rasp in my throat. I throw myself from side to side. No help. I've tipped the chair over. Just what I need right now.

"Well, that was not a very smart move, Mr. Fishbaum, was it? No need to spend your last minutes in such an uncomfortable, undignified position."

She motions to Mickey, who comes over and, without any effort, lifts me together with the wheelchair and sets me upright.

"I want to put your mind at ease, Mr. Fishbaum. I want to tell you that we are not heartless about the way we carry out our work. In a few minutes, I will give you a shot of a special cocktail that will help you sleep, the Big One, if you catch my meaning."

She leans the shotgun against the wall, reaches into a black leather handbag and removes a flat silver case.

Out of it she takes a large syringe and a vial. Fitting a thin needle to the end of the syringe, she sticks it into the vial, tips it up and draws out a whitish liquid.

"No ballistics, you see. No mess. All the real nasty stuff we'll do afterwards when you're no longer with us. For the photo shoot you understand. Need to have the proof the job has been done to the letter. Must be professional. I'm sure you'll appreciate that. We'll roll you over to the barn for that. Easier to clean blood off concrete."

Nice to find a killer with such consideration for troublesome household tasks.

Carrying the full syringe she walks across the room towards me.

"You'll feel a sharp prick and not long after a feeling of euphoria and then no feeling at all."

I can do nothing but watch death coming for me. I don't close my eyes.

What about Anna? She said they weren't going to harm the children. OK. That's good. Very good. Look for something, anything to hang onto. Her mother will come for her. She'll be fine. Anna will be fine. Anna will be fine. That's good. I can … No, I can't hear her and Harley outside. Can't remember when I last heard them. As if my thoughts had been intercepted, Minnie stops and turns her head towards the window.

"You wanna go out and round up those kiddies now?" she says to Mickey. "We needs to be getting on and getting away before it's too deep even for the four wheel drive."

Turning to us, she explains, "As you all will understand, we will have to take those two along with us. Insurance. But don't fret, we'll take real good care of them."

Mickey lurches up from the couch, goes out the door and into the yard. Still can't hear the kids.

"Darn," says Minnie, looking at me. "How am I going to give you a shot through that jacket."

She glances around, goes into the kitchen and returns with a black-handled knife.

"Anna, Harley," I hear Mickey call out. "Come on in now. Time for some nice hot chocolate."

Minnie sticks the knife in the cuff of the jacket and cuts up until the fabric is peeled back. She does the same with my shirt.

Outside Mickey calls out again, his voice more indistinct as he gets further from the house.

"There we are," she says.

Now I close my eyes. I can't stand the sight of needles going into flesh. I feel the needle against my skin. Even if I believed in God, no time for a prayer. I feel the promised sharp prick.

A loud metallic clatter, followed by a thumping, heavy clanging crash. Sounds like it's coming from the barn.

I open my eyes. Minnie has removed the needle. A trickle of white liquid runs down my arm, but I can see the syringe is still pretty full. Holding it, she rushes over and looks out the window.

"Now what the hell is going on out there? You all will

excuse me for a second?"

She puts down the syringe and collects the shotgun. Holding it leveled, she opens the door and takes an exploratory step outside.

I hear a tree branch snap. Then another. A sharp intake of breath, a grunt of pain and Minnie stumbles into the room and falls flat on her back. The shotgun drops to the floor beside her. Two sticks, no not sticks, two arrows, feathered ends and all, protrude from her chest. What? Norfolk Indians? Robin Hood more likely. She gasps, her back arches and a thick gurgle of blood gushes out from under the bottom of the mask.

"That's the lot of 'em, I reckon," a voice shouts from outside.

The doorway fills up with a broad-faced man wearing red suspenders and a flat cap. He's holding a crossbow in his right hand.

"Looks like we come at about the right time then, don't it?"

Under the Beet Pad

"They're safe and sound," says Fergus, thumbs hooked into his red suspenders. "Couple of the boys took 'em back to the caravans. Didn't want 'em round here 'case it went bad. Fact is," he snorts a laugh, "didn't want 'em here whichever way it went. Put 'em up on the big horse. They must a thought Christmas had come on early. Pleased as punch they was."

You never know what will save your ass. For me it was Gwen's goat. Not that it literally saved my ass. It was a more roundabout ass saving. Kevin, the boy who was wounded in the shotgun incident, was bringing fresh goat's cheese to Gwen's, a sort of reciprocal peace offering, when he saw her all beaten up and bloodied being dragged from the barn. Seeing that Mickey and Minnie were armed, he ran to get help. The men arrived to see us go into the house but were too late to warn us. They waited outside for their chance.

"Didn't want to put 'em down like we done, but figured with them having guns like they did, it were the only sure thing. First time ever used the bow on anything but muntjacs. Didn't know if I could, but when I saw her coming out with that shotgun, well, just let 'em fly was all. Sorry bloody mess, Paddy my boy. Sorry bloody mess."

The biggest mess was Mickey or what was left of him. He'd gone into the barn searching for the kids. Instead he'd found, or been found by, one of Gwen's large pieces of steel cut loose from an overhead gantry. Thankfully, I didn't have to see the body. A couple of the travelers had rolled it in a canvas tarp and stuffed it, along with Minnie, in the back of the killers' Land Rover.

"Appreciate what you done," Paddy says, shaking his head, eyes down. "Should never have let it happen like it did. Never should have done."

"How was you to know?" Fergus replies, settling his bearlike paw on Paddy's bearlike shoulder. "What was you to do, son? They was armed and with the shotgun up against Mrs. Gwen like it were... No. Nothing you, nothing no one could a done."

We're all in the kitchen. By the sink, Molly is gently washing the blood from her mother's head and face. One eye has come up black and yellow and is almost closed. I roll over, reach up to touch her arm.

"Gwen, I am so sorry about this."

"Shut the hell up!" Molly turns and yells at me with real venom.

The skin around her mouth is red raw where the tape's been pulled off, making her fury appear more ferocious.

"Sorry? Look at Gwen, will you. You think 'sorry' is going to fix this or all the rest of it? I'm the one should be sorry, sorry you ever moved in next to us, sorry we hooked up with a damn Yank hoodlum, sorry we didn't tell you to clear off when we had the chance."

"Molly," Gwen croaks, "leave him be. Please. It's not his fault. They were going to murder Bob. Remember? Only just stopped that women before she could inject him. They were planning to dismember him for Christ sake! Ouch! Hey, careful there, love."

"She's right, Gwen. Really she is. I should have taken off before, when that woman came looking for Anna. I'd left it too long. I was hoping, I guess, that I was, that we were safe. So listen, maybe it's too late, but now we're all still alive, it is really time to go."

"Wonderful," Molly snaps at me. "Really bloody wonderful. 'Time to go' is it? Fancy that. Go on then Bob. Go."

She's always called me 'Greenie'.

"Sure, go on, run for it and leave us simple-minded muppets to explain those two dead people and the guns. How the hell do you reckon that's going to work? No? No answer? Why am I not surprised?"

"Not to worry 'bout the bodies, Miss," Fergus says from the safety of the far side of the kitchen. "We're after digging out a piece of ground for Old Man Debbage for him letting us stay in his field till we move on in the Spring. Wants us to make him a beet pad. When the snow clears we'll dig down a few feet more, drop 'em in with some quicklime. Soon as it warms so as we can pour the concrete, they'll be gone good and proper. No one be the wiser."

"What about the car?" Paddy asks.

"Probably ripped off," I reply. "People like that won't want to leave a paper trail by renting or getting caught on close circuit.

"I think maybe then we're looking for a joyriders' burnout. Fergus?"

"We'll see to it, Paddy. Not a problem, especially after the other we got to do. Have one of the lads take her somewheres up the coast. Not many coppers around. Afore we do, you might want to have a look through their stuff. Couple of cases we found. Mobiles too, them fancy iPhone ones."

"Will you listen to yourselves," Molly shouts. "Just bloody listen. You're all making it sound so damn simple. Bury bodies. Burn cars. Poof. Just like that. Poof. Gone. Back to normal. Everything back to bloody normal. I'm telling you it won't go way. It will never go away. Someone will see something. Someone will hear something. Someone will say something. And then we'll all be in the shit. Shit!"

Paddy comes over and wraps his thick leather-clad arms around Molly. She swings herself around trying to shake him off, but he holds on as if his life depended on it, which it probably does.

"Take her easy, Molly. Come on now. Come on. We're all shook up real bad. Falling out with each other ain't going to help, is it?"

"Damn it, Paddy Driscoll! Just damn it, damn it, damn it to hell!"

Finally, she sags against him in defeat. Her body quivering with rage and despair, silently she weeps.

Blood Money

"You feeling any better, Gwen?"

"Terrible," she replies, her voice breaking. "My head is killing me and I am nauseous like it's never ever going to stop. When I close my eye I see those poor dogs lying there, crimson stains, really deep crimson ones, spreading out from their bodies into the snow. I couldn't make any sense of it. Then I saw them, those two people in masks, at the barn door. Mickey Mouse, Minnie Mouse, bloody hell! Oh, God but my eye is throbbing something awful."

She is lying on the couch, a bag of frozen peas on her eye. Her face is grey and she's looking ten years older. I am sitting on the floor, still feeling a tad high from the few drops of goodbye cocktail. I'm stroking Gwen's hand. Through to the kitchen I can see Paddy and Molly, arms interlinked. They are leaning across the table from one another talking in low voices. Fergus promised to bring the children in the morning. Gypsies. Horses in the snow. They're probably having a real adventure. Best of all, they're safe.

She'd been winching up a heavy piece of steel, the piece that a little later came back down in a hurry and put out Mickey's lights. The noise of the lifting chains meant she hadn't heard the car pull up. The first thing she did hear was the dogs barking furiously, three loud reports and then whimpering followed by a final report. Grabbing her just-cleaned shotgun, she rushed to the barn door to be met by the two loveable Disney cartoons, one of whom, she thought it was Mickey, slammed a pistol across her face.

"I suppose it's too late for the police?"

"Well past too late, Gwen. For one thing, Fergus has already gone off with their bodies. No way to sell that to the cops."

"Russians?"

"Don't think so. Hired by them, that's for sure."

"So, now there'll be others coming for you?"

"Don't know yet. Maybe."

"Bloody hell!"

"You bet."

"What can we do?"

"You mean, what can I do. No 'we' involved, Gwen. First thing is to find out who those two were and if they'd been sending info back to LA. I've got their cell phones, but they're code locked. Need to figure out how to break in. Nothing helpful on the bodies. No ID. Even labels were cut from their clothing. No credit cards. Nothing. These two were the real deal. Must have paid for everything with cash. Had a couple of thousand pounds between them. Gave it to Fergus for all the trouble. Pretty cheap I reckon for what he did. Might find something more on them when I'm able to open their suitcases. Waiting for Paddy to find a hammer and chisel."

"You know, I suppose I never fully believed you about all that gangster stuff. Thought you were exaggerating, making up a good story to impress. Silly me, huh?"

"Yeah, and stupid me for what's happened. Molly was right, I'm poison."

"Greenie?"

Paddy is standing over us.

"Here," he says, handing me a blue, rubber-handled mallet and a cold chisel. "You want me to do it?"

"Thanks, I've got it. Maybe hold the suitcase for me."

One strong tap and case one flips open. Inside are women's clothing, underwear, couple of skirts, blouses, a dress, makeup bag, nightgown. A leather folding case.

"Bingo! Here we are. A passport. No, two, no, three passports. US, Irish, Israeli. Airline tickets. Lisbon, Jakarta, Delhi. Each passport in a different name. No closer to knowing who she was. Could be any of these. Probably none of them."

Meanwhile, Paddy has popped open Mickey's suitcase.

"Same here. He's got four different tickets, four different passports. The same as hers, with a UK one as well. From his accent, I say for sure he was a Brit."

I lift the empty suitcase. Something's not right. Too heavy. I shake it. Nothing moving.

"Paddy, hand me that chisel, will you?"

I put the sharp end of the chisel along the top inner seam of the suitcase lining and pull it across. As I do, stacks of dollar bills wrapped in paper bands cascade out. I do the same on the bottom lining. More stacks of bills.

"Holy Mother!" Paddy shouts.

It's the first time I've heard anything like that from Paddy. He takes the chisel and cuts into the other suitcase. Another hoard of bundled dollar bills spills onto the floor.

"How much do you reckon?" he asks.

"Molly come in here and have a butchers at this lot."

She comes in and sits down on the couch next to her mother.

We stack up the bundles. I count out the bills in one, while Paddy counts the number of bundles.

"I got fifty 50s," I say. "Two and a half grand in each. Paddy?"

"Thirty. We got thirty packs. Bloody hell, that's $75,000! If we split this up that'll be more than enough to set up that tattoo parlour you always on about. Wadda you think to that, Molly?"

"I think this all is looking like big trouble," Molly says. "Big, big trouble."

"Not necessarily," I reply. "First off, nobody knows what's gone down or even that these two clowns, whoever they were, were here."

"You know all about this kinda thing then?" Molly asks, not trying to hide the bitter edge in her voice.

"Enough, Molly. Enough to know that, one, these were hired pros who don't leave footprints. Bodies, yes. Footprints, no."

"Leaving us alive," she shoots back, "that's a pretty sizeable footprint, wouldn't you say?"

"Which is why I'm now thinking that they probably had

other plans for you and the kids, although it might be like they said, one dead foreign gangster would be neither here nor there, but a mass killing would be much more risky than leaving witnesses who could only give the cops two Disney mice."

"Why all this cash?" Gwen asks.

"They didn't want to risk being tracked. Cards leave tracks. This is also probably the first installment on the hit. Once they let them know it's been done, they'll get the final payout, probably in a numbered account somewhere. Don't know if we'll ever find that out, but it would be best if we could."

"Won't that be risky?" Paddy asks.

"Yeah, maybe, but not finding it and not taking it out would be more risky. These folks were planning a hit and a quick exit. If this is what I think it is, they were independents who work through one, maybe a couple of intermediaries. They had a pretty good clue who they were working for, but nothing more than that. So, the Russians will not expect to hear directly from these guys, but will know something has gone wrong when the money is not collected."

Paddy studies the pile of dollars and then turns his attention to me.

"What about the too obvious fact that you're still alive? No body, no second installment. That and then another lot of villains sent over to shoot off your crippled arse."

"For once, I'm ahead of you on that one, Paddy. I've got a plan. Just need to pull it together."

The Big Ask

"So, Brendan, wadda you think?"

"I can do it, Bob. That's not the difficult part. As long as they open the email and the attachment, we're in. That's if they're the primary. They may be a cut off. But if they forward the email, we can most likely follow that. The other stuff you want, that'll be rather more of an effort. For that, we'll have to call in some specialist help. However, let's take it one step at a time. You ready?"

A hour or so earlier Brendan had got real excited when I told him that some unpleasant people, unnamed, of course, wanted to rub me out.

"Rub you out? Really? Rubbed out? A real live mob murder in Norwich? Not as if we haven't had too much of that already. 'Course those were only random Norfolk Nazis. You're talking about like gangsters, like in the films! Bloody Nora!"

My first thought, finally and completely abandoning my aversion to 'effing, was, fuck Coppola and fuck Scorsese. Yeah fuck the both of them. That was also my second thought. My ass is on the line and all anyone can think about, even the killers, is the god-damned movies. Besides, who needs movies. In the last few weeks I've seen more killings here in Norwich then I saw in all my years in LA. Of course before the Russian's muscled in the knockoff clothing racket wasn't what you would call heavy duty in terms of people getting wacked.

I told Brendan most of the story leaving out the

details of what happened out at Gwen's. What he does know is that I need the bad guys to believe I've been murdered. I also brought him Mickey's and Minnie's cell phones hoping he could break the four number code. He made a call and about twenty minutes later a bent over little bandy-legged guy, wearing a Hawaiian shirt and a Yankee's baseball cap, kinda slid in around the doorframe. He didn't say a word. Seeing the phones, he snatched them off the table and trotted to the far end of the room. Five minutes and he was back. He dumped the phones down in front of Brendan.

"That'll be twenty quid, Squire."

"Pretty steep for five minutes work," I said.

"Too fucking steep? Tell you what, how about I lock the fuckers up again? How's about that?"

I handed him a £20 note.

"See you in church, Hot," Brendan had called after him as he scooted out the door.

"Nice guy," I said

"Not really, but he is a wizard at what he does."

And now I'm sitting with a more friendly wizard ready to find out what the murderous mice have been up to.

"Fortunately, your friends don't seem to have been very sophisticated. Here, look at this."

On the computer screen are columns of email addresses against which are brief messages.

"Brendan, please, you wanna lay it out for me in English."

"OK. From what we got here, they've been sending emails every day to two different addresses. One day this phone sends to this address, the next day it sends to the other one. The other phone mirrors that. Also, look at the time. See here. There seems to be a pattern. Both phones send the same message, but more or less five minutes apart."

"A security thing? Like two launch keys for a nuke."

"Something like that. Pretty basic. Anyway, the recent messages themselves don't tell us much, but you can guess easy enough. 'Still looking for that coat you wanted'. 'Weather nice again, still no coat.' That's until a few days back, when we get 'Located coat. Right size too.' Then two days ago, 'Before purchase, please confirm size you wanted.' Return message says '42 long, as agreed. Don't forget pants. Send hard copy receipt in case returns needed.' My guess is that you're the coat. The pants and the receipt, don't know."

Lying bastards. Still and all, what the hell did I expect from a couple of hired assassin mice.

"Pants, I'm guessing that would be my daughter."

"You sure about that, Bob? Little Anna? Why would they want to do that?"

"That's how they operate. I told you they were vicious bastards, Brendan."

"No kidding. And the receipt?"

"Proof of some kind probably. Newspaper clipping, photograph maybe, although I'm thinking 'hard copy' could be an actual photo, not something sent by email. They might think that's too risky."

"In that case, Bob, we have more problems. We might

get away with sending another message off to them today. A holding message. You know, saying they're checking the coat to make 100% sure. But we'll need to get the mock up newspaper page done and a convincing photo and figure out where to send it. That's to say nothing about having to build the right kind of Trojan horse to plant on their computers and then planting it."

"A big ask, then?"

"No, Bob, more like The Big Ask. But after what you did for us, I'm more than ready to give it a go. I owe you."

And, of course, they all felt they owed me. Hedgy set up a wonderfully bloody spattered tableau consisting of me with chunks of raw liver and cow's blood decorating my head and in a corner, a more obscured body of what looked, even close up, like a small child.

Brendan easily got onto their computers, as his email with the Trojan horse attachment was passed though from one link in the chain to the next. Not only did he break in, but also managed to find a likely address to mail the eight by ten of Hedgy's handiwork.

It turned out that none of the mice's emails mentioned where we were or where they were. Security for them became security for me and Anna. So, Sylvia wrote an article, together with three follow-ups, about the murder of an American tourist and his daughter. He'd been going by the name of Benjamin Gold, but the police discovered that his real name was Robert Fishbaum, a low-level criminal from Los Angeles. To cover our trail she set the killing in Liverpool, where there seemed to be enough violent crime that one more didn't make too much noise.

Sylvia said that Hedgy's stuff was too graphic, even for some of the ass-end newspapers, but when the bad guys got the photograph that should be good enough for them to maybe close the book on Bobby Fishbaum.

Brendan then did some fancy schmancy computer thing that meant when anyone using the Russian computers looked for the articles about the murders they would be automatically be redirected to the special Liverpool Echo newspaper he'd set up on his server.

"Not foolproof, Bob, but unless they start browsing the nationals, it should work. Of course, they may begin to wonder why the story never made the newspapers in Los Angeles. Afraid I can't crack that one for you."

OK, so that was that, as well as eventually they'd find out the second half of the payment hadn't been collected. At that point, hopefully, the trail will be stone cold. Anyway it's a risk Anna and I have no choice but to live with. As my old man used to say, "What is life without a little risk? Exciting like gefilte fish without the horseradish."

Now I'll just have to convince Gwen about that.

The End